TRIPLE DOWN

Muffin Top Bakery
Book 3

TASHA HART

Description

Description

Trulia Grant left the big city to find herself. Instead, she found a man who helped her discover a whole new world...

Trulia was always the runt of the litter. Out of the three Grant sisters, she was always the quirky one—*different*—and paved her own path no matter the obstacles in her way.

So, it wasn't surprising that she never expected to move back to her close-minded hometown, but that's not all she never expected.

She never expected someone like Tyson Hayes to enter her life.

This white boy is gorgeous, laid back, and has a quiet charm that pulls at her heart. Where Trulia thrived on the energy of New York City, Tyson has a laid back and easy going attitude.

He's not her type, and she's *definitely* not his.

But something brings them together and forces them to crave one another when they're apart.

Can these two figure out what is between them— if these feelings are real—before they get hurt? And hopefully before other people hurt *them?*

Chapter One

TRULIA

I wake up feeling refreshed and happy, perhaps for the first time since my mother died. Things with her death are finally wrapped up. The bakery is doing good, her estate is settled—things finally feel like they're going back to normal. Now I can actually just focus on the grief without all the extra stuff.

Mama and I weren't as close as my sister Bridgid was with her, but Mama *always* accepted me for who I was. She never judged me, always kept an open mind. Like when I decided that I no longer wanted to be called "Katrina" anymore and told her that I demanded to be called "Trulia." Mama didn't even argue. She just gave me a hug and nodded.

It's lonely not having that person to go to anymore. I've always been independent in my actions, and no one could ever tell me what to do or who to be. But when it came down to it, when I needed help or just someone to talk to about the serious shit in life—I called Mama. And now I can't.

I've been dealing with that ugly truth pretty well if you ask me—but it has definitely affected my art. You see, I'm a visual artist. I moved to New York City shortly after I turned twenty. In New York, I was always able to find some type of job where I could do what I loved. NYC has such a broad spectrum that I never had any trouble with that. But here, in small town Texas—it's much different. *Much* different. And the inspiration has been incredibly lacking lately.

That's why today I've decided to take a little trip to a nearby park that I've been eyeing. I do lots of different types of art—but my favorite thing to do is paint. More specifically, I like to paint nature. Sunsets, moonscapes, beautiful views, flowers etc. It's what I feel the most at peace doing. So when I'm looking for a little more inspiration for a piece, I like to walk around in nature and take pictures of things that I find beautiful. Then I can look through them when I get home and see if I like any of them enough to paint.

On my way to the park, I turn on my favorite R&B station to get myself into a more creative mood. Once there, I pull out my favorite and only professional camera and begin my walk. Luckily, it's a beautiful day, so it doesn't take long before inspiration strikes. I'm able to snap a couple good shots before my phone rings.

Ugh, it's James—my sort-of boyfriend back in New York. I say sort of because we aren't technically official—meaning we're both allowed to see other people (which I know he does).

The arrangement seemed fine at first—no strings or feelings involved. But James seems to like the no-commitment thing a bit too much for my taste. I kind of thought that by now we would've turned into something more. So lately when he calls, it takes everything in me not to just decline the connection.

"Hey babe, what's up?" I reluctantly answer.

"Hey Tru, it's been a minute since I heard your voice. It almost seems like you're busier now than you were in The Big Apple."

My mother just died, you dipshit—of course I've been busy.

"Yeah, it's been a little crazy. But things are settling down now."

"Oh yeah? How's the small-town life treatin' you?"

"Oh you know, it's pretty boring. Not really my style, as you know."

"Yeah, I'll bet. When you comin' back to the city? It misses you."

"I'm actually not sure right now. Something seems to be pulling me to stay here a bit longer."

Awkward silence.

"So how have you been?" I ask.

"Good, good…"

"That's good."

Things seem to get more and more boring with each conversation we have. It's like without me there, we've just run out of things to say, or forgotten how to speak altogether.

"How are your sisters?"

"Good, they're good."

"No more screaming matches?"

"Oh no, things have calmed down a whole lot. They're both actually really happy right now."

"Sounds pretty boring. At least when they were screaming it was fun to watch."

"Yeah… I guess."

Awkward silence.

"You know, James—I'm actually in the middle of trying to find some art inspo right now. Could I call you back later?"

"Yeah, for sure. I got some stuff to do anyway. Talk later, bye."

"Bye."

I hang up, with no intent to call him back any time soon.

It's not that James isn't generally a nice, handsome man. He is, it's just that we aren't really on the same page in any aspect of our lives. He seems to be perfectly content with the "relationship" we have, and I most certainly am not. I'd rather be single than have something this meaningless.

So why haven't I ended it? Well, I keep telling myself that I shouldn't make decisions like this while I'm in the midst of my grief. Especially because I'm kind of known to be quite an impulsive person. I'm trying to improve on that part of myself. But truthfully, I know that I should end it. I'm not really sure what's keeping me from doing it.

After our phone call, I just feel even more lonely than I did beforehand. As I'm encroaching on thirty-four, I find myself craving a real partner. Something more. Especially after seeing both of my sisters fall in love in less than a year.

I'm honestly a little jealous of them, and maybe even a little sad. For the first time probably ever, all three of us are getting along perfectly. And at the same time, both Bridgid and Regina have found the men of their dreams, leaving me even more alone. It's just my luck, too. There's nothing worse than watching everyone around you being perfectly happy when you're the most miserable you've ever been.

Stuffing my camera back in my bag, I give up and head back to my car. I'm certainly in no mood to be doing this now, I'll have to try again tomorrow.

Chapter Two

"Alex come on man , we were just here last night," I say with a hint of annoyance, as he pulls into the parking lot of the local pub.

"That was a full twenty-four hours ago dude. Besides, what else is there to do?"

He's kind of right...

Alex has been my best friend since childhood. We've stuck together through everything, and I mean *everything*. We're thirty-four now and *still* best buds—how many people can say that?

To be fair though, we live in the smallest town in Texas ever to exist. Okay, I'm sure that's not totally true, but it's pretty damn small. You really don't have many options for friends here, so you might as well keep the ones you've got.

So why am I annoyed? Well, Alex is a real drinker—like, he could stay at the bar all night long kind of drinker. He could sleep there, wake up, and have a beer for breakfast. Me? I'm good after about an hour—usually less.

We walk in to see the same crew that was here last night—even a couple of the men sitting at the bar look a little familiar. Sighing, I plop down at the same stools we sat on yesterday. Just another boring night in a town that never seems to change.

I know I sound like I hate it here, but I really don't. I love this town and the four or five shops it has to offer. It's just a bit repetitive for my taste.

So why haven't I moved if it's that boring? Well… where the hell would I go? Besides, all my friends and family are here. It's pretty uncommon for anyone here to move elsewhere—probably for that very reason.

"What can I get for you two handsome men? Same as last night?" asks a young bartender with a heavy southern accent.

"Yes ma'am—two tall beers to start please," Alex tells her with a wink—he's always going after the twenty-year-old's.

"Actually can I get a double shot of your finest whiskey straight?" I intervene.

"Sure can," she twangs, and turns to get our drinks.

"Whiskey straight? Damn Tyson, what's the occasion?"

"Oh just feelin' something a little different tonight is all."

As soon as she brings our drinks, I down mine and immediately ask for another. It's gonna be one of those nights, I guess.

Just as the bartender brings me my second round, the door to the bar jingles and a low buzz erupts—which usually means some women have walked in. So predictable. Rolling my eyes, I turn to look at what we're working with, and sure enough—two stunning dark-skinned women have entered, accompanied by two men.

I immediately recognize them as the daughters of the woman who opened up the only bakery within a twenty-mile radius. They're pretty well known around here—especially because they're some of the only people who actually escaped this town—I wonder what brought them back.

I recall them from my younger days. I'm a few years older than them, so I never knew them very well—but I do remember that they were always absolutely gorgeous.

I don't recognize the men they're with, and they definitely don't look like they're Texas natives—too pale. Regardless, those are two lucky men.

"Those are the daughters of Ms. Grant, who owned The Muffin Top," Alex whispers.

"Owned?" I question the past tense of the word.

"Yeah, she died a few months ago, practically the whole town went to her funeral. She was such a nice lady; it was very sad."

"Where the hell was I when this happened?"

"That was when you had to go up to Dallas for a few days for work."

"Ahh," I recall the only fun week of my summer. "That sucks—what happened to the bakery? I haven't been on that side of town in a bit."

"I believe she left it to one of the daughters. It's still up and running though, I go in there about once a week."

Peeking at the girls over my shoulder, I vaguely recall there being a third sister. Downing the rest of my drink, I wonder where she is.

"You want another?" Alex asks, flagging down the bartender.

"Nah, I'm actually gonna head home now, I've got a real early day tomorrow."

"For real? Damn, well you want me to drive you home?"

"No it's okay, I'm gonna walk actually."

I throw some cash on the counter and head out, feeling slightly guilty for lying to him. I don't actually have an early day tomorrow—I just couldn't handle yet another night sitting in the same bar, talking about the same old stuff.

Walking through the town after taking four shots of whiskey makes everything look slightly more beautiful. Maybe that's why Alex drinks so much—it makes everything just a tad more interesting.

I decide to take a little detour, passing by The Muffin Top Bakery, which is closed for the night. It must have been real hard for those girls to lose their Mama like that —I don't know what I'd do without mine. I feel a pang of sadness in my heart just thinking about it.

Finally, I reach home. I'm hit with a wave of loneliness as I walk into my empty, silent house. I don't mind being on my own, but after a while it does start to get to you. It isn't easy coming home to no one every day—especially when you thought you'd be coming home to your own little family by this point in your life.

Falling into my bed, I'm able to shove down that lonely feeling and bury it for now. But as I drift off to sleep, I'm not sure how much longer I'll be able to ignore it.

Chapter Three

TRULIA

Today I wake up two hours before I normally do so that I can shower, throw on some clothes and head out before anyone else wakes up. Lately I've been feeling like I don't really belong at the house. It's Reggie and Michaels place now.

Honestly, I just kind of feel like a stranger here, like an invisible third wheel. It's not that I'm not happy for them, I'm not a monster—of course I'm happy for my sister. It's just really lonely for me. And today I just don't want to deal with that and sulk around in my loneliness all day long.

I've been considering what it would take for me to get my own place, and if that would even be worth it. It's not like I have to worry about my apartment back in New York, because I've already sublet it to a nice young man for the month. So I've decided to throw my all into putting together some new pieces in my hometown—the place where I first discovered my love for the arts.

Yesterday's endeavors were kind of a bust, so today I'm taking a different route. Before bed last night, I came up with this fantastic idea involving a tree sculpture. It actually came from a picture I took at the park yesterday but painting it didn't really feel right. I stared at it for hours thinking about what I could do with it, and finally I decided that I want to give it a more physical form. So today I'm going to go searching for some things I can use to create my sculpture.

I hop in my car and drive around kind of aimlessly for a bit, while I stuff my face with a banana nut muffin I swiped from the kitchen on my way out. I'm not really sure exactly where I want to go or what I'm even looking for, so I drive over to a small creek I know of and park on the side of the road. Grabbing the bucket that I always keep in the back of my car for scavenging—in case inspiration strikes—I head into the trees.

I walk up and down the creek for about an hour before giving up and plopping down on the bank. Taking off my shoes and socks, I let my feet dangle in the water. I prop myself up on my elbows and close my eyes.

I listen to the sounds around me and go over the things I can feel and hear. I hear birds chirping, and the sound of water running. I feel the grass scratching at my arms and the water rushing over my feet. Branches and leaves swaying in the wind. Squirrels running through the grass and the wind against my face.

This is something Mama and I used to do all the time growing up, just the two of us. Now it's something I do when I'm feeling a bit blocked. She'd take me somewhere, anywhere, and she would have us sit down, close our eyes, and recite everything we could feel or hear. Some of my best memories with her are from those moments.

As I got older, those were usually the moments when we would have our deepest conversations. That's when we'd talk about boys, or art, or school, or my dad. Those moments were just ours, and no one else's. I've never even told my sisters about them.

It takes a minute for me to notice the warm tears streaming down my cheeks, but once I do, I let them flow. I haven't really let myself cry since Mama left us. Every time I start to feel sad, I shove it back down and distract myself with something. Looks like I'm running out of things to distract myself with…

I roll over onto my stomach, bury my face in my arms, and sob. After a few minutes, I wipe away the tears and sit back up.

Mama would have loved this little spot, and I wish she were here. I tell myself that wherever she is, it's a hundred times more beautiful than this, and I know that she's out there somewhere closing her eyes along with me.

Just as I'm starting to feel a little better, my phone rings. It's James.

"Hey babe," I answer, trying to sound chipper.

"Hey sexy, watcha doin?"

"Just trying to find some inspiration for a new project."

"Well then that's exactly what you're about to get," James says.

"What do you mean?" I question.

"Well, I was actually calling about the gallery where you always display your art at."

"What about it?"

"Well… I just passed by, and they're currently showing someone else."

My heart can't help but sink a little knowing that that should be me.

"Damn, well it was only a matter of time I guess."

"I just thought maybe that might help give you a little motivation to come back home."

"James, I told you I can't leave yet."

"I know, I know. I'm just trying to make you miss it is all."

"Believe me, I miss it every single day. That's not what's stopping me from coming back."

"I'm sorry babe, I wish none of this happened and everything was back to normal."

Feeling the tears creeping back in, I feel the need to end this call.

"I'm okay, I promise. Look, thanks for that information—I think I know exactly what I need to do for my project now. You actually helped, thank you, James."

I hang up before he even has the chance to respond, grab my bucket, and run back to my car. I know what I need to make my sculpture and that's metal. I start up my car and make my way to the railyard to see what I can scavenge there.

Chapter Four

TYSON

I wake up in a panic, thinking I'm late to work—only to realize that I don't even work today. One of the drawbacks of working in such a small town? Not a whole lot of work to be done. The handyman business isn't exactly booming—in fact, it's extra slow these days.

I tumble out of bed and throw on my running clothes. Running has always been something I've enjoyed. Most mornings I run about five miles (at least). Today I set my goal for a solid six miles and head out. Running is kind of my way of keeping myself active in this boring small town. I almost never take the same route, and I never stay in Belton. I usually just run until I'm lost and then turn back around.

Today's weather is perfect for my run—sunny with a slight breeze. I used to try to get Alex to run with me, but he was never as committed to it as I am, so I always just ended up waiting around all morning for him to just not even show up. I got my little brother into it and he came with me almost every day for a couple years until he got married and had a baby—now he doesn't have time for anything, much less running.

Once home, I head straight to the shower. As I'm washing my hair, I wonder what the hell I'm going to do today. I mull over my options before I settle on going out to the local rail yard to collect some scrap metal. I've been scrapping metal as a little side gig for quite a while now. It's what I end up doing most days to make some extra money, among a few other side jobs.

After my shower, I decide to cook up a nice big omelet for myself. Six eggs, two different kinds of cheese, some spinach, maple flavored bacon, onions, and some tomato and avocado on top.

'*Man do I need a lady I can cook for,*' I think to myself.

I down two glasses of orange juice and devour my omelet before I'm officially ready for the day.

This is actually how most mornings go for me. Wake up at six, run, shower, eat, and go. It's a nice little routine I've gotten myself into. Keeps me from slipping into a depression, which I'm more prone to these days.

Heading out for the day, I start to feel another wave of loneliness. Sometimes I feel like I'm wasting what could be the best years of my life all alone. But I've been finding it harder to open up to women these days. It's just hard for me to trust people after what happened in my last relationship. I mean, of course, we all have relationship baggage… but it's not all like mine to say the least.

Arriving at the rail yard, I get to work. After a few hours of loading up my truck, I finally take a break. Just as I find a little spot to eat the sandwich I brought for lunch; I spot a small car driving up. Not thinking much of it, I go back to my lunch.

A few minutes later I notice a short, dark-skinned woman wandering around the place. She has on these huge white sunglasses, a flowy boho-inspired dress, and bright white tennis shoes. Definitely not the kind of look you see every day.

She's wandering around with a medium sized bucket, surveying the yard, and occasionally bending over, picking some things up, and putting them into her bucket. I can't help but stare. It's not often I run into anyone here, especially not some random woman. I find myself wondering what the hell she could possibly be doing here—and what she's putting into her bucket… and why.

The more I stare, the more I realize that I recognize her. It takes me a moment to figure out from where, but after a while I realize that she's the third sister that was missing from the bar the other night. I remember her being the youngest, and the one I know the least about. She's definitely one of the sisters that left town shortly after graduating—there's no way I could miss it if she had been around all these years.

Now my curiosity spikes—this is such an odd place for her to be. I debate approaching her, but I've been watching her for so long now, and she definitely thinks she's alone—I don't want to scare her or creep her out.

Okay fine—I'm just nervous to talk to such a gorgeous woman. Even from here I can see how stunning she is. Anyone with eyes would find this woman attractive. I wonder whether she's single or not. I even find myself getting a little turned on looking at her curvy figure. I have to snap myself out of it and refocus myself on my lunch and the reason I'm here.

I finish up my sandwich and try not to stare, which gets increasingly harder. Her long straightened black hair flows around her in the wind, sort of like a lion's mane. She looks like she just walked off of a photo shoot set.

I feel some sort of pull to this woman, I honestly don't think I've ever set my eyes on a more beautiful human being, almost like an angel. I start to wonder if maybe

I'm hallucinating, and she isn't actually real, until out of nowhere she turns her head and looks right at me. We lock eyes.

Fuck.

Chapter Five

TRULIA

I head from the creek to the rail yard, determined as ever. Before I'm even there, I feel like I may have found the perfect place to find what I need for my sculpture.

Now all I need to do is find a place to actually work on this, since Mama's house is *definitely* out of the question. Maybe I can rent out a small space for the time being, until I'm ready to go back to New York.

It's about a ten-minute drive from where I'm at to the rail yard, and the bakery is in the complete opposite direction —so as much as I love Bridgid's coffee—I stop at a small café along the way. I always feel a bit guilty getting coffee or baked goods from anywhere else when I'm in town. Mama's probably glaring down at me right about now.

I realize after slurping down my cappuccino that I'm *starving*, but it's too late to go back and get something to eat, so I continue on my way. It's not long before I'm pulling up to the rail yard. I grab my bucket and set to find what I need with laser-like focus.

When it comes to my art—once I've got an idea-,there's no stopping me. I almost become completely oblivious to everything around me. Which is probably why I didn't notice him at first.

After a few minutes of searching the grounds and putting random objects into my bucket, I start to feel a tingle of awareness. The hair on the back of my neck stands up, and I immediately whip my head around, only to lock eyes with a very tan, very tall man.

He's standing across the yard from me, staring me down. I stare straight back, which would cause any sane person to look away, but he doesn't. He continues to stare at me, unblinkingly.

I feel a surge of panic, wondering if maybe I'm not supposed to be here. That feeling quickly passes, as I realize that I've never seen any signs around here saying no trespassing. After a moment I decide to approach him —at the very least, maybe he works here and can point me in the direction of some better materials for my piece.

As I make my way over to him, he doesn't look away. The closer I get, the more I notice how beautiful this man is. Dark, almost black hair, freckles, and piercing blue eyes. Not to mention his body… this dude is *ripped*.

I turn my focus back to his face as I get closer, so he doesn't think I'm staring at his body. He leans against what appears to be an out of commission rail car. Damn, he's sexy.

'Don't drool, Tru,' I tell myself.

When I'm almost directly in front of him, I flash him a smile.

"Hello, my name is Trulia—do you work here sir?" I ask.

He reaches out his left hand to shake mine, which is when I notice the small tan line around his empty ring finger.

"Tyson. I don't officially work here; I'm just collecting some scrap metal. Did you need some help?"

His bright blue eyes are almost mesmerizing as the sun twinkles down on them. It takes me a second to realize he's speaking to me.

"Actually, yes! I came here looking for some metal pieces for a project I'm working on," I show him what I've collected so far in my bucket. "I don't seem to be having much luck though. Do you know of a better area I can search?"

"Well, what exactly is this project of yours?" he questions.

"Umm, it's kind of hard to explain, and I only just decided on using metal for it today, so I'm not *exactly* sure what it is I'm looking for. You see, I'm an artist—I'm not sure that it's going to make much sense to you, plus I'm really bad at explaining things."

"Try me," he says, a small smirk forming on his face.

"Okay… um, well I'm trying to find pieces that I can use to build a sculpture. It kind of formed from this picture of a tree that I took-" upon hearing him chuckle, I stop. "I know it sounds weird, I told you I'm not very good at explaining things."

"No, no! I don't think it's weird—it's just—trees are made out of wood…"

"You think it sounds dumb? Oh maybe you're right—I've been so out of it lately and this was the first real idea I've had in months."

"No, it sounds very interesting. I'm sorry, I didn't mean to sound rude. So let me get this straight—you want to make a tree sculpture out of metal?"

"Yes…"

"Well, then you came to just the right guy. As I said, I'm here collecting some scrap metal. I've already been here for a few hours, so I've gotten some pretty good pieces so far. They're in the back of my truck if you want to sort through them and see if you like any of them," he offers.

"Really?? Are you sure you don't need them for something? I don't want to mess up all your hard work."

"No, absolutely not. I come here a couple days a week, so I always get the best pick. You're absolutely welcome to come back to my truck with me and take a look."

"Well… okay, if you're sure."

"Not a problem, let me just grab my stuff real quick."

It's not until he turns to grab his things when I realize that this guy could be some kind of weirdo. Should I really be following some stranger back to his truck? My sisters would kill me if they were here. Despite my newfound worries, when he turns and motions me to follow him, I don't hesitate. Something about him just makes me feel like I can trust him.

Chapter Six

TYSON

The moment she got close enough to see, the first thing I noticed was her beautiful hazel eyes. I couldn't take my eyes off of them. Light green, with a hint of light brown and even some yellow specks. I've never seen more beautiful eyes in my whole life. This woman is definitely an angel.

The more she talks, I realize that she is not like anyone I've ever met. Everyone around here is honestly kind of the same in one way or another. But everything about her is different. Her looks, her outfit, her interests, the way she rambles… it's all very unique, in a good and exciting way.

She just so happens to be here looking for some scrap pieces of metal to use for a project she's working on, and I happily invite her to come check out the haul I've already collected today back at my truck.

I'm parked all the way across the lot, so there's plenty of time for me to make some small talk and try to figure this girl out.

"So, you're one of Ms. Grant's daughters, aren't you?" I ask, even though I already know.

"I am actually! How did you know? Were you at her funeral? I don't remember seeing you there, but then again that day was kind of a big blur."

"Oh no, I was out of town when that happened. I just remember seeing you back in the day, you have the kind of face one doesn't forget."

Fuck. I didn't mean to say that—it just kind of slipped out. Hoping she doesn't notice; I try to cover it up by continuing.

"I was very sorry to hear about your Mother—I'm deeply sorry for your loss. Your Mama was a very important woman in this town. Practically everyone knew her. She'll be missed for a very long time."

"Thank you, that's very kind of you to say. Did you know her?"

"Not personally, but I've been to that bakery more times than I can count. She would always let me try free samples of whatever she was baking in the back."

"Yep, that sounds like Mama for sure. She was always such a generous person. She must have liked you if she let you try free samples though—she doesn't give those out to just any old person."

"Well, consider me honored," I shoot her a smile.

"I really appreciate you doing this for me—I haven't had much inspiration to start up a project since Mama passed. This is the first time I've even had an idea that I liked enough to try to bring to life. I know it doesn't sound like anything big, but it's something, ya know?"

Before I can respond, she rambles on.

"This is obviously my hometown, as you know—but I've been living in New York City for almost fifteen years now. I make my living there off of my art pieces. So being back here has been a real downer for me, and not just because of Mama dying. I just want to get myself back into a decent groove."

Man this girl sure likes to talk.

"Well that's understandable you know—to lose motivation when something tragic like that happens. Your mind is so clouded with everything going on that it's almost impossible to even *think* about anything else," I finally get a word in. "That's perfectly normal. All that matters is that you're at least trying."

"Yeah, so you get it. But I told myself that this is what Mama would want me doing, you know? She wouldn't want me to sit around on my ass wallowing for months on end. She would want me to take that grief and turn it into something good. She would want me to use it for my art. So that's exactly what I plan on doing."

"That's good—a lot of people wouldn't be strong enough to do that. I know she would be really proud of you."

"You're right… she would be," she says with a soft smile, more to herself than to me.

Trulia definitely doesn't seem at all like my usual type—but for some reason, something about her just pulls me in like a moth to a flame. The energy around her is just exquisite and makes me smile.

Something about this girl's unusual, quirky style makes me want to get to know her, even though we only just met. I feel like maybe we were meant to run into each other today, and that's a very weird feeling to have.

As we walk to my truck, dodging pieces of metal and rusty machinery, she continues to ramble on about this sculpture she is planning to make with the metal. I still have absolutely no idea what she's talking about or how she could possibly turn this junk into something beautiful

—but she seems to know exactly what she's talking about, so I don't comment on it.

Finally, we reach my truck. Trulia goes silent as she runs up and immediately starts digging through my collection. She turns to me, eyes lit up, with a huge smile plastered across her face.

"Oh my god, this is *perfect*! You have no idea. This is going to be so great. Everything I could possibly need is here!"

My heart warms at the sight of her looking so giddy. I now know that this was absolutely supposed to happen. Even if the only thing that comes from this encounter today is that I helped her out with her art project—I'll be content with that.

Chapter Seven

TRULIA

Something about this man just calms me down and makes me feel like I can trust him. Maybe that's why I talk his ear off the entire walk back to his truck. We talk about Mama, and I tell him about my art and what exactly I'm planning to do with all this metal to turn it into a sculpture.

I can see that he's a bit skeptical about me using metal for this, like he's underestimating the magic that artists can do. We can turn pretty much anything into a work of beauty. He just needs to be shown that is all. And I plan to do exactly that.

Finally, we reach his truck, and my jaw drops to the ground. I run up and start looking over everything in a frenzy. This is even better than I could've dreamed… looks like running into Tyson is turning out to be exactly what I needed today, in more ways than one.

On top of helping me, Tyson is the first person I've come across since coming back home that even slightly interests me. I can't pinpoint exactly what it is about him that's interesting, but I can tell that there's definitely something in there that's different from the rest of the locals, and I want to find it.

It definitely doesn't hurt that he's fucking gorgeous. I've never met a man that still looks *this* good even after working out in the hot sun all day. Not to mention his body is as toned as it could be. I can almost count his abs through his baby blue t-shirt that almost matches his eyes perfectly.

He's definitely the most attractive man I've ever met in my hometown. He's got that kind of hot farmers' son thing going for him, even though he's not a farmer. I have to hold myself back from reaching out and running my hands along his chest and arms. I feel a little tingle in my lower stomach just thinking about how good those hands would feel running along my body.

A slight pang of guilt shoots through my chest when I remember James back in New York, waiting for me to come home. Even though James is just a "casual" thing —I still feel bad for lusting over this other man.

I mean, James and I have been very vocal with each other that our relationship is open and there are no attachments. There is absolutely no doubt in my mind that he is so *not* the man I want to spend the rest of my life with. If Mama had met him, she would have been so disappointed in me. He's exactly the kind of guy she warned us to stay far away from.

It's not that he's a terrible guy or anything. He's pretty average as far as looks go. He's not a bum, he's polite to strangers. It's just that he's kind of a player... and he doesn't have much of a brain if I'm being completely honest. I could never see myself committing to him, and I think he probably feels the same way about me. We've always been on the same page about that.

I know I should probably just end it with him already, but I guess I've just been scared to be completely alone during this period in my life. There's just been a lot of changes happening way too fast, and James is the one thing in my life that has remained the same. I kind of wanted to keep it that way until I became a little more stable. But staring at Tyson and his many many abs—is starting to make me rethink that.

I bring myself back to reality, focusing on the task in front of me—which is *not* Tyson.

As I'm digging through the bed of his truck, I've fallen completely silent—which I'm sure he's relieved about. I'm determined to get everything I need so that I can potentially start this thing tomorrow. Pretty soon I've filled up my entire bucket, so I hop into the bed and begin to hand Tyson different pieces. I have no idea where he's putting them, and I don't care—I am completely in the zone right now.

After about a half hour of sorting through his truck, I decide that I've probably found enough to make my sculpture. Besides, if I end up needing anything else, I can just come back and look around some more. I hop out of the truck to be met with a huge pile of scrap metal, and Tyson standing next to it.

"Wow… I guess I didn't realize how much I was grabbing—this is a lot…" I say, cringing inside. I feel bad that I've basically just stolen all of this man's hard work. What if he needed it for something?

"Look, I can put some of this back, I feel bad…"

"No, no don't be ridiculous. You don't need to put any of it back. I'm just happy to help."

"Are you sure? Thank you, you're an incredibly generous person."

"Well, I did grow up in Belton," he says, gesturing around him.

"True, this town sure has taught us to be pretty selfless."

"So do you want to go back and bring your car on over, and we can load it up?" he asks.

"My car... oh my god, I don't know why I didn't think about this before... but I might actually have to give some of this back to you after all. There's no way I could fit all of this into my tiny car."

I put my hand to my forehead and begin pacing back and forth in front of the pile, until I feel Tyson's large hands clamp down on my shoulders.

"Tell you what—why don't I put it back in my truck and I can just bring it to wherever you need it?"

"Really? Oh that would be great!"

I rack my brain thinking of a place where I can tell him to bring it, only to realize that I don't have one yet.

Damnit.

Chapter Eight

TYSON

Seconds after I suggest that I can take the metal in my truck to wherever she wants it at, her face falls. She looks crushed, defeated. She almost looks as if she could cry.

"What's wrong??" I question her.

"Um… I'm sorry to do this but—I don't actually have anywhere for you to bring them. I don't know why I didn't think of this before. I'm currently crashing at my Mama's house where my older sister is staying with her new boyfriend, and I can't bring it there—there's no way I could work on my project there. I'm so sorry to have wasted your time…"

The poor girl looks so sad, I can't bear to watch her leave like this.

"Wait—um, I actually have my own little warehouse. I only use it to store my tools and such, but for the most part it's a pretty open place. It might be the perfect place for you to work on this if you're interested…"

"Oh, no—I don't want to intrude. I can just leave the stuff here, find a place to rent out and then come back and get it, it'll be fine."

"If you leave all this perfectly good metal sitting here, someone is bound to scoop it right up. These are quality pieces right here. Trust me, you don't want to leave it here—it'll be gone when you come back."

"Well, I guess I can bring my car around and just try to load it up with as much as I can, and then you can take back the rest. I doubt I'll need all of this anyway."

"Now why in the hell would you do that if I'm offering you to come use my warehouse. Look, there's no harm in at least checking it out. If you see it and you don't think it's the right place for you to do this at, then that's fine. But at least you'll have looked."

"It's not that I'm worried the space isn't right—in fact, I'm sure it's perfect. It's just that you've already done so much for me today, and I don't even really know you. I would feel so bad."

"The only reason you should feel bad is if you let my perfectly good warehouse stay as empty as it is. I promise you, all I use it for is my tools. Tools that you might even be able to use to help with your sculpture. I'm hardly ever in there. It's all yours if you want it. Last call."

She seems to mull it over for a minute or two, before finally coming to a decision. A cute little smile spreads across her face as she looks back up at me. All of a sudden, she runs and jumps into my arms, hugging me.

"Thank you, thank you, thank you. You've saved me so much today, you really are my knight in shining armor, you know," she says as she hugs me even tighter.

As her body presses into mine, I have a hard time not thinking about her plump breasts pressing into my chest, or my hands resting on her waist just above her round ass. I have to snap myself out of it, so I don't get a hard on while she's hugging me.

Finally, she pulls away and I can breathe again.

"Why don't you help me load this stuff back into my truck, and then I'll swing around and drop you back at your car and then you can follow me to the warehouse?"

"That sounds perfect! You know, you're a real lifesaver. Do you treat every stranger you come across like this?" she asks, a soft twinkle in her hazel eyes.

"Not all of them," I reply with a sly look.

"Guess you're like my Mama in that way."

"Alrighty, let's get to work now," I say, giving her a playful push. She giggles, and we begin loading the metal back into my truck.

Once we're finished, we hop into my truck and loop around back to where I first saw her tiny red car pull up earlier. Seems like forever ago that I first spotted her. Guess a lot can happen in an hour.

"Alright, just follow behind me. It's not too far!" I shout as she makes her way to her car.

"Okay! See you there!"

I find myself smiling practically the entire drive to my warehouse. Something about this girl…

I can't help but think that someone must have hurt her pretty badly in the past. She obviously isn't very used to kind gestures, and I wonder when was the last time anyone did anything nice for her just because.

I'm low key hoping that her using my warehouse for her project will result in a lot of bump ins between us, so I guess the act wasn't *totally* selfish. I can't help it; this woman is having some sort of effect on me. I just want to know more about her. Hopefully, this will give me the perfect opportunity for that.

The excitement in me builds up as she follows me through town. I try to tell myself to calm down—that I don't even know if this woman is single or if she is even going to be interested in me.

By the time we reach my warehouse, I've completely talked myself down and forced myself to stop thinking about her in that way. Or at least I tell myself I have.

Chapter Nine

TRULIA

As I follow Tyson to his warehouse, I can't believe my luck. Things like this never happen to me—nothing ever goes my way.

Should I be skeptical that this stranger wants to take me back to his empty warehouse? Yes. Am I? No, because for some reason, Tyson doesn't seem like a stranger to me. He almost feels like an old childhood friend whom I've known my whole life and have finally reconnected with.

By now I probably sound like this careless, damsel in distress who just trusts every person she comes across. But I promise I'm not. I've lived the past decade of my life in New York City, which is full of weirdos. But this is Belton. It's different here. And Tyson is different.

I recall back to when we introduced ourselves and I noticed that he had no ring on his finger while we shook hands. Instead, I noticed a fading tan line around where a ring used to be. I catch myself wondering what the story is there. Probably divorce. Divorce rates are pretty high in Belton. No one ever stays together.

It must have been a while ago, considering the way he reacted when I hugged him. He seemed really taken aback and his whole body stiffened a little—everywhere. I can't really blame him—I shocked myself when I went in for that hug.

After about a ten-minute drive, we arrive at his warehouse. It looks extremely well-kept; you can tell that he cares about the place. I park my car while he opens up the warehouse door and backs his truck into it so that the bed of the truck is just inside.

"It'll be easier this way for us to sort through everything. Now you don't have to hold back, take whatever you think you might need for it. Anything you don't end up using, I'll just scrap."

"Wow, this place is nice, how long have you had it?"

"About seven years now. It was my dads before that, but he retired and didn't need it anymore, so he gave it to me. I don't use it too much, but my dad spent so much of his life in here that I feel like I have to keep it nice for him. He actually built the place completely from scratch all by himself. When he dies, it'll be like having a piece of him still with me."

"Wow. I can understand that. That's what the Muffin Top is for my sisters and I. Mostly Bridgid though."

"Is she the one who took the place over?"

"She is! Although, she kind of took over the place well before Mama got sick. Bridgid has always been Mama's little clone. Her baking is *amazing*."

"That's awesome, I bet your mother loved to watch her follow in her footsteps."

"Hell yeah she did—if Mama had it her way, we would all be working in that bakery full-time. But Regina and I never really got into the whole baking thing. Regina's more of a cooker, and me? Well, I just eat everything they make."

Tyson laughs, and he has this sort of throaty, sexy laugh that makes you wish you had more jokes to tell.

"What does your dad do? You said he spent all of his time in here?"

"Yeah, dad was a carpenter. The best in town. He was amazing. But it aged him a lot, so he had to retire early. He's not really in the best shape now. I do a lot of handiwork, but my little brother is the one that really followed in his footsteps. He's at the top of the carpenter game now. Dad's real proud of him."

"So why didn't your brother take this place?"

"Well actually, for my fathers last project before retiring, the two of them built him his own warehouse. It's pretty cool."

"Wow, that's amazing. I can't believe he built this place all by himself," I say, looking around me in awe. There even appears to be a small loft above the common area.

"Yeah, he's really talented. It was really sad when he had to retire. I know he still misses it. He practically lives vicariously through my brother."

Tyson and I continue to chat and get to know one another while we sort through all the scraps.

"Did you always know you wanted to be an artist?" he asks me at one point.

"I did, actually. Bridgid was always the baker, Regina was more into school—and I was always off creating something. I don't know what I'd do if I couldn't be an artist anymore."

"Why'd you move to New York? Why didn't you stay here?"

"Honestly? Reggie had already left, and I just felt like there was no way I could spend my entire life in this small town. I knew that I had to get out there and explore."

"I get that. I kind of wish I had done that. Do you think you'll ever come back?"

"You know, I always said that when I was ready to settle down with someone and start a family, I'd come back here so that I could be near Mama and my kids could know their grandmother. But now that Mama's gone, I don't know. It might be kind of sad if I came back."

"What would your mom want you to do?"

"Oh she would want me to come back, without a doubt. She always said the city was no place to raise a family, and that she knew I'd be back at some point."

"Mother knows best."

"That she does. Is your mom around?"

His face lights up at the mention of his mom.

"She's my best friend, literally. My mom and I have always had such a special bond. I have so much respect for that woman."

"Aww, that's so sweet. It's nice to hear a guy talk about his mom like that for once. You don't hear that too often."

"Yeah well, not everyone is blessed with a mom as amazing as mine."

"Please tell me you don't still live with her," I joke with him.

"Oh god no! I don't love her *that* much. Honestly, Trulia —I'm offended!"

There's that sexy laugh again that I can't seem to get enough of.

We spend the rest of the afternoon laughing and getting to know each other more as we sift through metal and find pieces for my sculpture. I can't even lie—it's the most fun I've had in ages.

Chapter Ten

TYSON

Once we've sorted through all of the scraps and put aside everything she is going to use for her sculpture, Trulia runs and grabs her sketchbook and some drawing pencils from her car—apparently, she doesn't go anywhere without them just in case inspiration happens to strike.

She spreads some papers out on the ground and gets to mapping out a few designs for her project. Occasionally, she gets up and walks over to the pile of scraps, stares at it for a minute, and then goes back to sketching. I'm very impressed by her determination for this. She is obviously extremely passionate about what she does; I can tell that she is completely lost in her own world and has forgotten that I'm even here.

An hour goes by, and she's still scribbling away. I wasn't sure if I should leave and just let her be, but I wasn't exactly ready to go back home yet to my empty, quiet house. So instead, I've been tinkering around with the leftover scrap metal and clearing a bit more space for her, since I'm sure she'll need it.

When it begins encroaching on the two-hour mark, I start hearing her stomach growling. I don't think she even notices it, and if she does, she definitely doesn't plan on doing anything about it.

I take it upon myself to slip out of the warehouse and order two pizzas for delivery—one cheese, and one pepperoni in case she happens to be vegetarian. I don't say anything to her, not wanting to disturb her focus.

The pizza arrives quickly, and she doesn't even notice me going outside, chatting with the delivery boy, and bringing the pizza back in. After a couple minutes, Trulia seems to come back to reality.

"What on earth is that delicious smell?!" she exclaims, getting up and running over to where I've set up the food.

Her face lights up when she sees the pizzas, and she grabs one from each box and lays them on top of each other, creating a sandwich. Before I can even say a word, she devours both slices.

"Um—I got both cheese and pepperoni in case you were a vegetarian."

"That's very kind of you. I could never be one though, Reggie would kill me. Besides, Mama always taught us to take any food that was offered to us and not complain. I didn't defy her then and I certainly don't plan on defying her now."

"Smart woman. How's the sketch coming?"

"It's going to be a couple days before I can start actually building it, that's for sure. I'm on my third sketch right now. This is probably the part that takes the longest. I have to make sure that I have everything mapped out perfectly before I begin. It's the only way."

"I'm impressed. You really love doing this, don't you?"

"You have no idea. Hey, what do I owe you for the food?"

"This ones on me," I assure her.

"Aw shucks, you didn't have to do that Tyson, seriously."

I did though, because I can tell that her stomach appreciates it as she devours slice after slice.

"You know, if you're not careful—you're gonna starve to death while working on this project of yours."

"Trust me, it wouldn't be the first time I've lost a few pounds while working. Sometimes my passion for completing a project and getting the vision just right, kind of makes me forget about any and everything else in the world."

"Wow—that's true dedication. It's amazing that you have something that you love to do *that* much. Not a lot of people have that, you know."

"Do you?"

"Eh, not really. I like doing handiwork and stuff, but I don't really have anything that makes me completely forget about the world like that. Except maybe running."

"Running? Like, for fun?" she questions, and I notice her eyes running over my body.

"Yeah, I go for a run every single morning, rain or shine. At least five miles every day. When I run, I definitely forget about everything except pushing myself to keep going. I don't know what I'd do without it."

"That's interesting. I've actually never met anyone that enjoyed running enough to do it just for fun. How long have you been doing that for?"

"Practically my whole life."

We continue to chat as we feast over the pizzas, which are quickly disappearing between the two of us.

"So where did Trulia come from?" I question her peculiar name.

"Well, actually—by birth name is Katrina. But around the time I was in high school I decided I wanted to be called Trulia. I really liked the idea of being able to choose what I wanted to be called for the rest of my life. When I moved to New York, I learned that it's actually very common for artists to create their own name. I know Mama secretly hated it at first, but I think once she realized it wasn't some phase, she finally accepted it. She never tried to stop me though. Some people call me Tru, for short. Either way works for me."

"You just keep getting more and more interesting," I blurt, without even realizing it.

My face immediately burns red, and Trulia emits a soft, shy smile in my direction.

As we polish off the last slices, we remain silent, while sort of peaking at each other every now and then. When I catch her staring at my lips, a sort of shiver runs through me and my desire flares.

As if we both sensed something in the air, we both stand up at the same time to clear up the food, but instead we bump right into each other. Me being much bigger than her, I send her flying.

I quickly catch her by the shoulders and steady her. The feel of her skin under my palms sends another shiver through me, and this time I can't ignore it. I find myself staring into her hazel eyes and leaning into her.

Fuck it.

Like a man dying of thirst, I lean down and kiss her, her lips a crisp glass of water against mine. We gulp each other down like we haven't had anything to drink anything in years.

Nothing in this world could have prepared me for the passion surging between us.

Chapter Eleven

TRULIA

'*He definitely caught you staring at his lips,*' I tell myself. My face heats up and I look in the opposite direction. I just met him, and I don't want to make things weird between us.

To avoid any more awkwardness, I stand up to clear away the mess we've made while eating. Unfortunately, it seems that Tyson had the exact same idea, so we slam right into each other, causing me to practically fall over.

Tyson clamps his hands down on my shoulders, steadying me. The hair on the back of my neck stands up at the feel of his hands against my bare shoulders. Suddenly, my stomach is full of butterflies.

I stare up at him, my eyes getting lost in his blue irises that remind me so much of the ocean. He stares back into mine with such intensity that it takes everything in me to keep myself from toppling over. A sexy, almost nefarious grin spreads across his face just before he leans in to kiss me.

The minute our lips touch, I feel like I've come alive for the first time ever. We devour each other as if we're starving, despite having just stuffed our faces full of pizza. My hands are equally as desperate, as they run along his taut arms, feeling every single curve and muscle they have to offer.

Feeling the need to be closer, I press my body into his. My nerves crackle, as if they've just been electrocuted. Any and all sane thoughts fly right out the window, and all I can think about is how I don't want this to end. I'll do anything to have this moment last forever.

Tyson grabs my hips and pushes mine into his, where I can feel how hard he's getting. A soft moan escapes me as his hands trail back up my body, where he then runs his fingers through my long, silky hair. He gives it a soft tug, pulling my neck back a little.

At this point, I just want to take all my clothes off for this man and let him have his way with me. I can only imagine what those giant bear hands could do to me, and he seems to somehow already know what I like.

His hands slowly move from my hair to my ass. Taking handfuls of it and squeezing, he presses me into his hard cock even more. From there he explores my body until he reaches my breasts, lips still grasping mine. I'm not wearing a bra, so when his fingers graze my erect nipples, I all but melt into his arms.

I moan against his lips, wanting more. His hands never stay in one place for too long, tantalizing me, teasing me. I would say he's doing it on purpose—but sensing his urgency I think it's more likely that he just wants to touch every inch of me.

His hands begin to slow down, becoming less urgent and more appreciative as he moves back down to my ass. He takes another handful, slowly squeezing it harder and harder, while using his grip to grind me into him.

Just when I'm about to say, "fuck it" and pull my dress off, he slowly pulls away and rests his forehead against mine, catching his breath. I can't help but feel massively disappointed. I don't think I've ever wanted something more in my life.

As we catch our breath together, I can feel his walls slowly coming back up. Whatever came over him to make him kiss me, is—for whatever reason, far gone. He slowly pulls himself away from me, avoiding eye contact.

Not wanting to press him or make him feel awkward, I turn back to my project, without a word. I can hear him shuffling behind me.

"Look, I'm sorry about that," he starts.

I turn around to see him leaning against the wall of the warehouse.

"Tyson, there's absolutely nothing for you to apologize for."

"I know—it's just—I shouldn't have grabbed you like that."

"Why not?" I question him.

This seems to stump him, and his brow furrows.

"Like I said, there's nothing to apologize for," I smile at him, trying to put him at ease.

He smiles back and nods, seeming to believe me. I know there's something going on in that head of his, something he isn't saying, but it's certainly not my place to question him about that. Whatever issues he's dealing with inside have nothing to do with me.

I begin working on my project again, as if nothing even happened. In the back of my mind, I question myself about what just happened. I only just met this guy, and I'm already throwing myself at him? What the hell was that all about?

I stop myself before I start to go down some shame spiral. I've always been very open with my sexuality, and I believe that we do what makes us feel good, and there is absolutely nothing wrong with that.

If it's consensual, and it feels good—who the fuck cares? Besides, there's something sexy about a woman who knows exactly what she wants and doesn't feel bad about it. Tyson definitely seems like he isn't used to a woman like that, and I'm almost positive that he's sitting over there going down his own little shame spiral.

After a few minutes, I get back into my groove of sketching out my design, forgetting about Tyson completely.

Chapter Twelve

TYSON

Still recovering from the kiss that just occurred, I sit down at my work bench while Trulia dives back into her project. Never in a million years would I have imagined that happening.

That kiss was so intense, I can't help but be a bit shaken up. I don't think I'll ever be able to forget how her lips felt against mine. Naturally, I feel a bit ashamed of pulling her in like that—but she seems to have moved on from it just fine, so I quickly banish that feeling.

Trulia is sprawled out across the floor, scribbling away, seeming to have completely forgotten what just happened. I on the other hand, don't know if I ever will.

The feeling of her skin against mine, her body pressed into me—her lips working away at mine—it was pure ecstasy. I have to fight with the part of me that wants to go over to where she's working and kiss her all over again, this time resulting in much more. I hold back, reminding myself that I only just met her this morning.

The air in the room isn't awkward or anything—it's just quiet, as if nothing ever happened. As if I imagined it. Though the fact that my cock is still hard tells me that I definitely didn't.

I think back to my ex-wife, Lindsay. I never felt anything like this with her. At the mere thought of her, my hard on instantly vanishes, and it's as if someone has dumped a bucket of ice on me. Probably for the best.

I try not to think about Lindsay too often, it's much too painful when I do. Lindsay and I were married for three years, and together for four. Yes, we got married after only one year of knowing each other—but trust me, that's normal here in Belton. Even still, one year is definitely not long enough to get to know someone before committing the rest of your life to them—so I guess you could say I kind of did it to myself.

Suddenly I begin to panic, and I can't get my mind off of the subject. This is why I tend to just banish any and all thoughts of my marriage—because every time one or two sneak in, my entire day is ruined.

I decide it's time for me to go home. Now that the memory of my ex has ruined my mood, I just feel like going home and crawling under the covers.

"Hey, I have a job to get to in a few, so I'm actually going to head out now," I tell Trulia as I grab my keys. "There's a spare key right outside in the green planter so you can just lock up whenever you're done. And feel free to use any of my tools over there if you happen to need any."

She barely looks up and sends a little wave in my direction, so I head out the door. I don't actually have a job to go do, so it looks like it's going to be another early night in.

Once I start my truck and get on the road, I'm finally able to breathe for the first time since that mind-blowing kiss. I can't help but replay it over and over in my head throughout the entire drive.

Once home, I plop down on the couch and turn on some TV. But for some reason, my mind wanders back to Lindsay.

I must've kissed Lindsay a million times throughout our entire relationship, and I can honestly say none of them were *ever* as electric as the one I just shared with Trulia. Everything with Lindsay was very textbook. There was no passion, no urgency. It was very bland.

'Maybe that's why she cheated,' I think. *'That's still not a valid reason though, because I was feeling the same blandness, and I didn't go outside of our marriage.'*

So why did we get married if there was no passion? I ask myself that every single day. I honestly think that we both just felt like it was the right thing to do. And it's Belton, there really isn't much else here. Both of our families got along, my parents loved her, her parents loved me. Our schedules fit together; our goals appeared to be the same. You could say it looked good on paper.

I think both of us were just scared that we would end up alone, and we were both encroaching on thirty. In Belton, if you're not married by thirty, you're pretty much alone for life. I think we just couldn't see anyone better coming along. At least I couldn't—I really can't speak for her.

I'm not saying it was all bad—the first year of our marriage was good. We bought our own house together; we were very happy and still very much in the "honeymoon phase". But honestly? Even our honeymoon stage was passionless. Dry, if you will.

During the second year, we were starting to grow apart. We barely talked anymore; the house was very silent. We would go months without having sex sometimes, and when we did have sex, it was almost like we were waiting for it to be over the whole time. It's not that we weren't attracted to each other. Lindsay is a very beautiful woman. It's just that there has to be more than basic physical attraction for you want someone like that.

After a year of barely talking, not going on any dates, and avoiding each other—I think we both realized that we had made a terrible mistake. The only difference was that I wanted to try to see if I could fix it—I wanted to at least *try* and figure out what went wrong. And Lindsay—well, Lindsay was already checked out.

She would say she wanted to try, but it turns out she was actually going out and sleeping with other men. We started fighting nonstop, so much that I never even wanted to be home. I would take as many jobs as possible, no matter how far away they were. Sometimes I would be gone overnight, and I guess that's when she would bring the other men home.

One day, I was supposed to be gone on a job, but the client canceled on me last minute, so I reluctantly went back home—only to find her screwing some man on our bed. I was completely devastated. I knew that our relationship was doomed—but I never could have guessed that she would betray me like that.

The worst part is that she wasn't even sorry for doing it. She was just sorry that she got caught. Who knows how long that would've gone on if I hadn't caught her. I packed up all of my things the very next day and crashed with Alex until I found another house to rent.

We were divorced within five months of that day, and all of that was about a year ago now. So yeah, it's really hard for me to think about—and I haven't been with another woman since. Can you really blame me?

Chapter Thirteen

TRULIA

It's been six days since I met Tyson at the rail yard, and I've been spending every day in his warehouse working on my project. It took me three days to get the final sketch, so over the past two days I've begun the first steps of actually creating it.

We've got a pretty good routine going. I wake up at seven, shower, eat breakfast—or not—and rush over to start working by eight. From the moment I arrive, I'm deep into my work until about two, when Tyson makes me get up, go outside, stretch, and at least drink some water. Then I get back to work, and around five or six he comes back and makes me go outside and eat some dinner.

During the times when he makes me go outside, we talk. We talk about everything—from our childhoods, to our favorite television shows. I talk about Mama a lot, and he listens. He's a good listener. I like those moments, but that doesn't mean I don't rush back into the warehouse to continue working on my project once they're over.

The first couple of days he would leave and do a job in between coming back and making me eat. But now that I'm actually building it, he likes to stick around a lot and watch. He's even been teaching me how to use a welder, which has been amazing for my project. I cannot thank him enough for his help, or even express how much joy I'm feeling now that my vision is finally coming together before my eyes.

Today I feel a bit more relaxed, I'm not in a huge rush to get straight to work after we have lunch. Of course, there's still lots of work to be done on my sculpture, but now that I know my project is going to turn out pretty much the way I want it to, I can slow down a bit and really take my time.

Neither of us have mentioned the kiss since that night, it's almost as if it didn't even happen. I still think about it though. When he isn't looking, my eyes trail along his toned body. I catch myself staring at his hands when he's trying to teach me stuff—not because I'm watching what he's doing, but because I'm remembering the way they felt clutching at my body.

On my drives home at night, I fantasize about kissing him again. I tell myself that I should just do it. It felt good the first time—so why not?

After we finish dinner—barbecue for the third night in a row—we sit outside talking, as we watch the sun setting. Normally, I'm back in there working already—but tonight I asked him if he'd sit with me for a bit longer.

Tyson really is a beautiful man. As the sun drifts lower in the sky, the light hits his eyes perfectly. His freckles are prominent. I've never met a grown man who still has freckles before. It's adorable.

I reach out to touch his cheek, admiring his beauty, before I even realize what I'm doing. He doesn't startle, he just looks at me. We stare for a second, before I stand up and walk into the warehouse. Tyson follows, closing the door behind us.

We stare at each other for another moment, before meshing together just like we did the first time. The minute his lips hit mine, it's like déjà vu. The passion is still there, maybe even more so now.

He grabs me and pushes me against the wall, with just a hint of roughness. I rip off his shirt, throwing it across the room. Running my hands down his chest and across his abs, my breath hitches—he feels even better than I could've imagined.

I slowly begin kissing my way down his neck, until I reach his stomach. I look up at him as I unbutton his pants and rip them off along with his boxers. His large cock springs out, and once again this man has shocked me. I've never been with a man so big, but that doesn't stop me from taking him in my hands and massaging his length.

He groans, pressing his palms into the wall in front of him, giving me even less space, as I'm sitting on my knees in between him and the wall. I run my tongue up his cock until I reach the tip. I put my mouth on him, sucking only the very tip as I watch his face. He grimaces, and I know he wants more.

"Fuck me," I tell him.

He starts to grab me to pull me back up to him.

"No," I say. "Fuck me."

I press the back of my head into the wall and put his dick inside my mouth, looking to him to see if he understands. His eyes widen for a moment as he gets it.

I put my hands up in the air, surrendering myself to him. He begins to fuck my mouth, slowly at first so that I can get used to it. Then he plunges all the way in, and his balls smack against my chin.

All I can think is '*Thank god I have no gag reflex.*'

His pace quickens, becoming more and more urgent, and I know it won't be long before he comes. He reaches down and grabs a tuft of my hair in each hand, as he fucks me harder and harder. Right before he's about to finish, he makes to pull himself out, but I stop him, grabbing him from behind and pushing him so that he's all the way down my throat when he comes. I shake my head slightly back and forth, enjoying it, before letting him pull himself out of my mouth.

I'm barely on my feet again before he rips off my dress, revealing my panties and no bra. He rips them off, literally, and turns me around so that I'm facing the wall.

"Oh god yes," I murmur, knowing what's about to come.

Needing no time to recover, he plunges himself into my already soaking wet pussy. I can't help but scream out as he enters me—I've never taken anyone this big before. He grabs my wrists and pins them behind my back, before proceeding to literally fuck my brains out.

"Please—don't—stop-" I pant in between thrusts.

He lets my wrists go and grabs a fistful of my hair, yanking my neck back and towards his chest as he fucks me. It doesn't take much longer until my whole body tenses up, my eyes roll to the back of their sockets, and I'm practically screaming as I come on his dick.

"That's right, baby, come for me," he whispers in my ear.

He holds me from behind as I experience the best orgasm I've ever had in my life.

He carries me up to the small loft above the warehouse, and we collapse on the bed, immediately falling asleep.

The next morning, I wake up in a panic, forgetting for a moment last night's events. After a minute, I remember where I am, glancing over at the naked man lying next to me.

"Good morning," I whisper.

"Morning," he says, staring straight at the ceiling.

I prop myself up on my elbows and shoot him a puzzled look.

"What's wrong?" I question him.

"Look, last night was amazing and I—um, I don't really know how to say this. I'm just not ready to rush into anything right now. My wife-"

"Your *wife*?!" I shout, shooting right out of bed.

"*Ex, ex-wife!*" he sits up, realizing how he must have sounded. "I have an ex-wife. And it's only been a year since the divorce and I-"

"You're not ready."

"Exactly! I'm not ready," he repeats.

"Well you should've thought about that before sticking your dick in me last night, huh?" I shout, wrapping the blanket around myself and running down the stairs.

I grab my clothes and quickly throw them on, heading for the door.

"Trulia, wait-"

"No, Tyson. I have to go. You may not be ready to confront what you feel between us—but I'm not willing to just ignore it. I see nothing wrong with what we did. There's nothing wrong with acting on how you feel."

With that, I grab my keys and rush outside, starting my car and driving off.

Chapter Fourteen

TYSON

As each day goes by, I replay what happened over and over again, trying to figure out what exactly went wrong. Trulia seemed extremely mad when storming out. I feel bad for telling her I wasn't ready after the fact, but I didn't *know* I wasn't ready. I didn't know.

It's not that the experience with her was bad—it was the best sex I've ever had in my entire life. And falling asleep beside her was even better. But when I woke in the morning, I felt empty. I felt ashamed for letting my emotions and attraction get to me like that.

I have never had sex with someone so soon after meeting them, it's not what I do. I wasn't thinking about it that night though, all I could think about was my need for her. It was like something came over me.

My hope right now is that Trulia doesn't feel like I used her. It was the opposite of that. When I think back to that morning, I wish I had gone about that conversation completely different than I did. I shouldn't have thrown that right at her as soon as she woke up.

Right now I'd do anything to go back and change that. I feel horrible about the impression I must have made on her. I feel even worse that she hasn't been to the warehouse to work on her project since that day, knowing how much it meant to her and how excited she was to do it.

After about a week goes by and still nothing, I can't take it anymore. My conscience is telling me that I have to do something—at least give her a proper apology. I just can't leave it like this. I decide to make a plan.

I spend my day mulling over what I could do or even say to make her forgive me and come back to work on her sculpture. After a couple hours, nothing comes to mind. I head out to my car and get on the road, no idea where I'm headed.

First, I stop at a local fast-food drive-through, ordered three roast beef sandwiches, a chicken sandwich, and two orders of curly fries dipped in cheese. Parking my car in a random parking lot, I scarf every last bite down.

When I'm done, I continue to drive around aimlessly. Next thing I know, I'm turning down the street that the Muffin Top is located on. I find myself driving extra slow, taking my time as I pass by.

My heart all but skips a beat when I spot Trulia sitting behind the counter with one of her sisters, having a good laugh together. Proceeding to speed back up, I drive all the way home without stopping once.

Maybe the bakery just needed help this week, and that's why she hasn't come by.

Ah who am I kidding. Whatever excuse I try to create, I know deep down that the reason she hasn't come by is because she's avoiding me and will probably never going to speak to me again. I wouldn't speak to me either—so I really don't blame her.

It's hard for me to admit, especially since I only knew her for one week, but I miss Trulia… a lot. I miss her quirky style, her peculiar sense of humor. I miss the routine we had going, that made me feel like maybe I could actually have a family one day.

I miss her unique way of viewing the world, family, and love. I truly have never met someone that interesting. Everyone I've met throughout my life, they always seem like they're trying to fit into some mold. But not Trulia. Trulia is her own mold, separate from anyone else. She's special.

I should have told her *that* the morning after we had sex, instead of talking about my ex-wife and scaring her off. I guess this is what happens when you go this long without dating.

At home, I lay outside in a hammock that I have tied between two trees in my backyard. I stare up at the sky for another two hours, just watching the clouds go by and the sky getting darker minute by minute.

Finally, I know what I have to do. I have to text her, it's as simple as that. I just have to text her, and say something, anything. That's better than this deafening silence that I'm sure is only driving her further away from me.

It takes me a whole extra hour to figure out exactly what I am going to say. I'm so nervous that it takes about six rewrites until I'm ready to send it. It reads:

Trulia. I'm sorry that it took me this long to reach out after that disastrous morning we had. I want to talk with you. I don't want to say too much in this text, because I would rather speak to you in person. All I will say is that I hope you will give me a second chance. I will be at the warehouse all night. If you decide you want to talk, you know where to find me.

My heart skips a full two beats as soon as it sends. I take a deep breath, before leaving my house again and heading to the warehouse to wait and see if she comes.

Chapter Fifteen

TRULIA

Tyson and I haven't spoken since our fight… which was now a full week ago. I've pretty much just been helping out at the bakery since—I haven't even gone back to the warehouse to get my things.

My sisters have no idea what happened or really who Tyson even is, which I'm glad for. I don't want them to make me talk about it and turn it into a whole big thing. Although, knowing my sisters—they definitely know that something is up with me. Surprisingly, they haven't questioned me even once, and I'm proud of them for that. Maybe they're just too wrapped up in their own nauseatingly happy lives to care.

I've been driving Bridgid absolutely bat shit crazy trying to get her to let me spruce up the bakery. She keeps telling me that she already did spruce it up right after mom died, and maybe she did—but it still looks so drab to me. I've been *begging* her to let me repaint the walls something brighter and happier, but she just shoves a cupcake in my mouth every time I try to bring it up.

Needless to say, all of us are going insane having me hanging around the Muffin Top. But I refuse to be the one to reach out to Tyson. Of course, I miss him, and I wish the fight hadn't happened. But I don't regret having sex with him. And the way he reacted the next morning made me feel like *he* regretted it.

I'm very open with my sexuality, which I assumed he had noticed by now. When I choose to be intimate with someone in *any* way, I never look back and regret it. Because I believe that when you feel something and you act on it, that can't possibly be a bad thing. I just don't like to shame myself about any of those things, and I wish other people didn't either.

So it's difficult for me to receive the backlash from someone who regrets sleeping with me, which Tyson clearly did. I understand his point about not being ready after his ex-wife, and I would *never* pressure someone into being ready. The thing is, he *did* make the conscious choice to have sex with me, and so clearly, he was ready —even if he wasn't ready to *admit* that.

I just don't want to be a part of whatever he is going through right now, because it has nothing to do with me. I have my own issues and things that I need to focus on without someone else dragging me into their stuff.

I'd be lying if I said I didn't miss him though. Of course I miss him. I think about him practically all day throughout my shifts at the bakery. I just can't seem to shake the thought of him.

I'm pulling a late shift today with Bridgid, and it's almost closing time when my phone chimes. I practically leap across the bakery to check it, hoping like I do every time that it's Tyson. Just like how every time the front door jingles, I hope it's him walking in.

Only this time, it really is him. He wants to talk in person and asks me to come over to the warehouse tonight. I immediately grab my purse and my keys, throwing off my apron.

"Hey B can you close alone tonight? I have to do something."

"Sure!" She shouts from the back room, not even bothering to come out.

For a split second, I consider making him wait a bit. But then I think to myself—why? I'm not ashamed of how I feel and I'm not going to hide the fact that I've been missing him.

I run out to my car and race over to the warehouse, where I can see Tyson leaning against the wall outside. I barely have the patience to turn my car off before hopping out.

Once I'm out of my car, I take a deep breath and force myself to calm down. I remind myself that although I want him to know how I feel—we still had a fight the last time we spoke, and I don't want him to think that that whole thing was okay.

Without making eye contact, I slowly make my way towards him, my anxiety building with each step I take. I'm suddenly more nervous than I've ever been around him before. What if he doesn't want to make up? What if the reason he wants to talk is to tell me that he doesn't want to have me in his life anymore, and he's kicking me out of his warehouse completely?

I quickly shake those thoughts out of my head as I approach him and finally make eye contact, shooting him a soft small. The energy between us is awkward and unsure.

Chapter Sixteen

TYSON

The moment my phone beeps with the text from Trulia, I feel myself tense up. I'm not sure why. I'm the one who has asked her to come, after all. The fact that she hasn't answered to tell me if she is coming or not is just making me more anxious. Wringing my fingers with each other, I look out the window at the dying sun.

"Gosh, what am I doing?" I ask myself, running a hand through my hair. I lean back against the headrest of the driver's seat. I know I wasn't ready for any of this before, and I'm still not sure that I'm totally ready, but I want to try.

Hell, I have to try if I don't want to lose her.

Closing my eyes, I see her anger on the back of my lids. It hurts me. I don't want to see her like that again. I don't want to be the reason she's upset. The other day was all my fault. I'm ready to move on from it if she's willing to.

I have this hope that she wants to move on too. I know it may just be some pipe dream, but I hope it's not. Trulia's the most exciting person I've ever met, and even the short time I've been without her has affected me.

I feel myself sinking again. I want to float back to the surface, walk on water with her. I pull my car key out of the ignition and stuff it into my pocket. I look down at my clothes for a moment and futilely dust them off twice before moving to finally get out of the car.

Swallowing nervously, I step onto the front part of the building and wait for her.

Hearing the rev of an engine, I look up and see Trulia's car pulling into the parking lot. Relief fills me as she drives up and parks beside my car.

I don't think I realized how much I have missed her until this moment.

Still sitting in her car, Trulia doesn't eye me, but something in her lap. Her phone maybe? I can't read her face. It's this weird mixture of a tense and amused expression. Of course, for all I know neither of them could have anything to do with me.

I don't know why I'm getting all worked up about this. It's usually pretty hard for me to get anxious about stuff, being generally easygoing and all. But the longer she sits in the car without looking up, the worse my stomach clenches. A part of me wants to go and knock on the window, but my feet feel so heavy I'm cemented in this place. Finally, she exits her car.

Slowly, she walks up to me, without making eye contact. Her steps ease and click against the pavement.

After what feels like forever, her tenseness melts and leaves only a smile. Then she finally looks up at me and meets my eyes. Her grin stays.

As soon as she's close enough, I pull her into a hug, pressing her body against mine and breaking the ice. The absence I've been feeling since things went off the rails fades further and further away until it's gone, fully replenished by her touch.

She wraps her arms around me as well and pulls tight. Neither of us say anything for a long while. I wonder if she has missed me as much as I've missed her.

"Hey," I say.

"Hey," she answers back.

"I missed you." My voice is still quiet.

"I'm sure you did." Her usual snarkiness underpins her tone. "I missed you, too."

"When I drove by the bakery the other day, I saw you, but I couldn't say anything. I'm glad you came."

"Yeah, I guess I've been there lately instead of… instead of here. It doesn't really matter, though. That didn't have anything to do with you."

"Oh, it didn't?"

"No." When we're finally done, she pulls away first and sighs, looking up at me. Her smile grows. "Sorry, handyman. Did not have *anything* to do with you. Not one thing. You really should be less self-absorbed, don't you think?"

"I guess. I should work on that."

"Mmhm. Tell you what, though, those girls were driving me crazy. Regina said I was being *impertinent* to some of the customers. Why she couldn't just say rude, I don't know. I had to get out of there, so I was actually relieved when you texted."

"We can talk inside," I say to her, taking her hand. We walk into the warehouse and take a seat on the floor. It's cold but doesn't bother me the way it usually would.

"So," Trulia says, "What's this about?"

"I want to… I want to pursue whatever is between us, Trulia. I really do— even with the past I do. But I think I need to go slowly. It was only a year ago with Lindsay, and I'm still trying to get over that, but I don't want it to mean we can't try. Because I like you a lot, and I don't want things to end because of something like that."

"I guess we can take things slowly," Trulia agrees, her fingers drawing invisible circles in the ground. "I like you, too, Tyson. You're definitely quite different from other guys I've been with, but I have enjoyed the time we've spent together so far."

"Good, thank you," I say.

"And, well…" Trulia shrugs. "I mean, I'll only be here for a month, and then I'll be going back to New York. My apartment is being sublet for about that much more. Why not have fun for a little, huh?"

"A month," I mutter, every sense of a happy feeling leaving my body, crushed by her words. I guess I'd been wrong. I see what she's talking about now. I stand abruptly. Why did I even ask her here?

Chapter Seventeen

TRULIA

"I mean, I'll only be here for a month, and then I'll be going back to New York. My apartment is being sublet for about that much more. Why not have fun for a little, huh?"

As soon as the words leave my mouth, I see the look on Tyson's face and realize that he clearly thought this was going to be more than just a passing fling. No wonder he isn't the type of guy I usually go with.

"A month," Tyson mutters. His body instantly goes cold against mine. He slides himself away. And stands. Clearly, I've hurt his feelings. I didn't realize he thought this was going to be something long term. I mean, I have

James and then I live in New York. What could he have been expecting?

"Tyson," I say. "I'm sorry I… You thought this was going to be a long term?"

"I literally asked if we were going to be taking things slow, Trulia. What does slow mean to you?"

"I'm *an artist* who works in *New York*, Tyson… you thought I'd commute back and forth for a year? Do video chats?"

"I didn't know you planned on going back like that at all. You were here, doing your art, doing us. You never even mentioned it would only be until your apartment was free again."

"It didn't matter until now, I guess. How was I supposed to know you wanted to do something serious? I don't want to do anything like that right now. If you weren't so clingy, maybe we could have had some fun."

"Clingy?"

"Yes, clingy. I mean, who drives by someone's business just to see if they're there? You can't even be independent for a few days, can you? You were probably sitting by the phone like a puppy dog waiting for me to call or text."

"It wasn't anything like that at all. You're the one who led me on."

"I did not. I——"

"Don't worry about it, Trulia. I see where you stand. Just lock the doors whenever you're done." Tyson turns around and storms out of the warehouse. I hear his car door slam and then pull out of the warehouse lot and off into the street.

"I should've known," I say. "Stupid, Trulia. Of course he isn't the type for a casual thing. Why'd you even get involved with him? You would've been better off just finding a one-nighter on Tinder or some crap. Look at how the crap hit the fan now."

My heart is still racing as I stare at the cracked warehouse door. I close my fists together tightly as the anger works its way through my body. I can't believe him. I should've known this was going to happen.

Why couldn't he have known, though? I thought it was clear that I'm not the type for some Romeo and Juliet snooze fest. I live big, I live a lot, and I do it all fast. Leaning against the wall, I slide down to the floor again. This was not how I expected our conversation to go. I thought we'd talk and then just make the most of the month we have left.

I'm angry at Tyson, but I'm also angry at myself. Should I have been able to see this? I didn't come here just to cause trouble. I just wanted to make some art—and look where that's gotten me. I know I need to figure things out, but right now I just need a drink to drown myself in my sorrows for a bit.

Standing, I go over to the metal pantry cabinet and pull out a bottle of bourbon along with the stack of metal shot glasses. Even though it's just me, I don't see the point in going one cup at a time.

I walk over to the table and set the cups out in a line. Then I quickly fill them each to the brim. I down the first two the fastest, and then I start sipping, ranting while I'm at it.

"If Tyson would just grow up, we wouldn't even be dealing with this. He's too… gosh, he's like a child or something. If you want to kiss me, kiss me. If you want to blow me, blow me. Don't play like you're some good little boy and deny yourself what you want. Don't just make all of these assumptions about people. It's stupid. He's stupid."

As it gets dark outside, the word stupid and my drinking are the only constants. By the time the bottle's empty and I'm on a second one, it's not a surprise stupid's the only word I can remember enough to get out right.

When I'm done, I'm plastered, definitely in no condition to drive myself home. I glance at the bed in the warehouse for a moment, but then I decide I'll just walk. I don't want to sleep in those memory-stained sheets. It would only make me sadder and angrier to think about the short-lived nice times we enjoyed in that bed.

I take my car out of my purse— I mean my purse out of my car, and then I'm walking down the gravely road back home. I find myself humming a tune I can't place as I go down the road. It isn't until I'm almost home when I realize I could have just called someone to pick me up.

"Oh well now," I mutter as I struggle to put the key into the lock of the door to let myself in. With all the scratching, I'm surprised no one's come down to check for a burglar. Once I finally manage to unlock the door, I stumble up to my room, crawling more than I'm walking with my hands in front of me and balancing my body on the stairs.

Kicking my shoes off, I can't even imagine the mess I left at Tyson's warehouse tonight. At least I can just tell him he deserves it if he complains, the bastard.

As soon as my head hits the pillow, I'm lost to sleep.

Chapter Eighteen

Tyson

As soon as I wake up, last night comes flooding back into my mind before I even have a moment to get used to the morning light. The screaming, the pain. It takes everything in me not to just roll back over and fall asleep.

Instead, I get up as usual. I skip my morning run for the first time in over a year, going straight to the shower. I even skip breakfast, which I never do, because I simply have no appetite.

The argument with Trulia last night really upset me. I haven't been this upset since my divorce. On one hand, I can see that Tru is this amazing, unique, kindhearted person who I feel an immense, deep connection too. But on the other hand, I feel like I don't actually mean anything to her and that she's just using me. With those two things completely contradicting one another, I'm not sure which side to believe.

My relationship with Lindsay was a train wreck, and Trulia is the first girl I've met since her that gave me hope that I might be able to fall in love again. But after yesterday, it doesn't seem like Trulia wants any kind of relationship with me outside of sex and using my warehouse.

I want so badly to hear her out and get her side, but it's getting harder for me to do that as time goes on. The more I think about it, the more I convince myself that I need to walk away from whatever this is.

Despite how depressed I still feel, I just cannot sit in this house all day, so I set out into town, with no specific destination in mind. It's gloomy outside, matching my current mood perfectly. I flip on my favorite radio station only to turn it off a minute later, not feeling much like listening to music this morning.

I'm not sure why, but I take a different route than normal today, one that takes me right past the warehouse. Good thing, too—because when I pass by, I see Trulia's car still there.

That's odd, she's never there this early.

I pull into the driveway to see what's up, which is when I notice that the warehouse doors are wide open, for anyone to walk right in. I still don't feel alarmed, Trulia probably left it open so she could work in the natural morning light.

It isn't until I step foot inside the warehouse that I realize I've been terribly mistaken. Inside, it's wrecked. All of my drawers are open, there's glass coating the ground, chairs knocked over.

Trulia!!

I frantically look around the warehouse, searching for her, thinking maybe someone broke in and hurt her when she was here last night. After searching every nook and cranny inside and out, I come to the realization that she isn't here.

When I walk back over to my tool drawers that are wide open, I realize that they're completely empty. Every. Single. One. It's in this moment that I allow myself to say what I've been too afraid to say since I walked in.

"I've been robbed."

I immediately pull out my phone and called the local police station. I give them some brief information, and they tell me to stay where I am and not touch anything, while they send a guy out.

My next call is to Trulia. Was she here when it happened? Did she get hurt? A million questions are running through my mind with each ring. After a few more rings, I get the voicemail. My heartbeat rises. What if something really did happen to her? I know it's only Belton, but there are bad people everywhere—I can't rule it out yet. I proceed to call her three more times, and it isn't until the fourth call that she picks up.

"Trulia??! Trulia are you okay??"

"Tyson? What's going on, it's like six in the morning," a groggy, half asleep voice groans out.

"Six in the—yeah I know it's six in the morning. I'm standing here in my warehouse that has been robbed at six in the morning."

"Wait what? What are you talking about?"

Seething with anger, I try to remain calm.

"You left the warehouse doors wide open last night… someone broke in and stole all of mine and my father's tools. The place is torn apart. The police are on their way. Are you awake now? Are you hearing me?"

"Yes, Tyson, I-"

"Good. Because now I am going to yell. How in the hell could you let this happen, Trulia??? You *know* how much this warehouse means to me and frankly, my whole family. I *trusted* you, Trulia! I trusted you…"

"Tyson… oh my god Tyson I'm so fucking sorry. After you left last night, I had way too much to drink. I was so drunk I had to walk home—I must have forgotten to lock up behind me. Oh god, I'm so sorry."

"I don't need your apologies. I don't think you understand. My *livelihood* belongs to those tools. Those tools will cost me hundreds if not thousands to replace. Without them, I have no way of making money. That was my whole source of income. Do you understand that??"

"I do, Tyson—I truly do. I'm sorr-"

"Stop. Your apologies won't bring back my tools. The cops just pulled up, now I need to go deal with this mess. Don't come back here."

With that, I hang up and go outside to give the police my statement.

Chapter Nineteen

Tyson hangs up on me, leaving me in complete and utter shock. That is, until the nausea hits. Now, the nausea is all I can think about. I ever so slowly sit up in bed, making it worse and worse.

Goddamn, this is one hell of a hangover.

And then I remember the phone call that just happened and how drunk I got last night. What the hell was that about?? I *never* drink that much, ever. And the one time I did—Tyson now has to pay for my mistake, immensely.

Words cannot even describe how badly I feel about this whole situation. I feel like my appearance in Tyson's life has just been like one big wrecking ball, and that all I've done is cause him pain and drama. I feel that he would be better off if I just disappeared out of his life. But before I can do that, I know that I have to fix what I broke.

I try coming up with a quick fix to this problem, but there isn't one. This is going to take more than just a quick fix, and I know exactly who to go to with this. My sisters.

I make my way out of my room, to find the house empty. Must have been an early morning at the bakery for everyone. I jump in the shower, washing away all of last night's stench. After I'm clean, I sit there, letting the steaming hot water hit my back. I sit there for quite a while, a few tears escaping every now and then.

What has my life become? How am I going to dig myself out of all these holes I've put myself in.

Once I'm showered and dressed, I head to the bakery without even so much as a glass of water. As soon as I walk in, Reggie and Bridgid rush over to me.

"Tru what's wrong?? You look beat." Bridgid says.

"Come on, let's sit you down. B go get her something to eat and drink, and some aspirin too."

I sit down at one of the tables, letting Regina hold me until Bridgid comes back. I take a bite of a buttery croissant, take the aspirin, and chase it with some coffee. My sisters watch me closely, waiting for me to talk.

"I've been sort of seeing this guy. Don't say anything. anyway, his name is Tyson, and he's such an amazing person. From the moment we met, he's been incredibly generous and caring. He's been letting me use his warehouse to work on my latest project. Well, last night we had this big fight, and then he left. After he left, I got really, really drunk—I know. I never drink, and with good reason. I had to walk home from the warehouse last night, and I guess I forgot to lock up the doors before I left. I just left them wide open. Tyson got robbed and it's all my fault," I confess, before sobbing into Regina's shoulder.

"Oh, Tru… Tru it's gonna be okay. I'm sure he knows you didn't do it on purpose. I'm sure he knows you're sorry. This isn't your fault, it's the robbers fault."

"No, it's *mine*. I did this. I've caused him nothing but pain since we met, when he's been so fucking nice to me. He's never going to forgive me, and I don't blame him."

"What makes you think he isn't going to forgive you??"

"He told me to never come back and then hung up on me…"

"Oh Tru, everyone says things in the heat of the moment when they're mad. I don't think he really meant that. Put yourself in his shoes for a moment. I doubt he's really thinking about anything else besides the robbery and the stuff he's missing, and then when it dies down, he'll be able to think about you more clearly."

"I don't know, maybe. But I doubt it. I'd be running the other way too if I were him, I'm a fucking mess."

"Tru don't say that. Come on, don't say things like that. Our mother just died; you have a right to be a little messed up right now. If he doesn't understand that, then he isn't worth your tears anyway honey. Now eat the rest of your croissant, you need it."

Maybe she's right, Tyson *has* to know that I've always meant well and that my intentions were never bad. He *has* to. And if he doesn't, well then, he wasn't paying enough attention to me when we would talk.

"Well, regardless of whether he forgives me or not, we need to come up with some kind of plan to get back all of the tools that were stolen. He worked so hard over the years to collect those, and without them he cannot do his job. I can't be the reason he's unemployed. We have to help."

"We will help, we will. We'll come up with something, we always do," Bridgid says.

The next couple of hours are spent consuming devilish amounts of cupcakes and various other sweets, while discussing what we can do to help, but not really coming up with anything concrete.

Suddenly, I remember how everyone in town came together to help us when Mama died, and we had to have that huge bake sale. I can't believe I didn't think of this earlier.

"I know what we can do, something that we already know will be guaranteed to make us enough money to help him. We will hold another bake sale, like the one we held for Mama. It went so well last time, better than we could've imagined. I know it will work again."

"You're right, that's genius!" Regina applauds me.

"We can make cookies in the shape of tools!" Bridgid brainstorms.

My sisters and I spend the rest of the day making plans for our bake sale. I know it will work because when the three of us get together, we always get the job done. Now all I have to worry about is whether or not Tyson will forgive me when all this is done, and if I even deserve for him to…

Chapter Twenty

TYSON

"Do you have an inventory of all of the items stolen?" the police officer asks me. His name is Tyler James Jones. He's holding a small notepad and pen out to write everything down. One page isn't going to be nearly enough. I had so much before the robbery.

"Um, well I don't have one of what was taken, but it was mostly everything. I have an inventory of what I had before, though. I guess that may be easier." I walk further into the warehouse and begin towards the back where my office is. I can't help but scowl when I see that nothing from Trulia's drinking was stolen, from the metal shot glasses to the sliver of whiskey left in one of the bottles.

Tyler James and I arrive in my office, and I sit down at my desk to unlock my computer. That's when I remember my computer was stolen as well. I bite my bottom lip to keep from cursing in front of the officer and stand again.

"That was on my computer, actually. Well, I should have a printed one in my files, but it won't reflect what I bought in the past week. I was going to update that today. Will receipts work?" I open the bottom drawer on one of my file cabinets and pull out the printed inventory, handing it to the officer.

"Hm," Tyler James says, looking it over. "It seems like they took all of your metal, even the small parts."

"Yeah," I answer dejectedly. "I don't think I'll be able to stay in business like this. I have nothing, and it's not as if I have the money to buy more or a way to make money to buy more." My business has basically been shot in the kneecaps by Trulia's stupidity. I run a hand through my hair and sigh deeply.

"Hey, I'm sure you'll figure it out, Tyson."

"I don't know," I say, sitting down at the desk again.

Tyler James takes a seat on the other side and begins copying items down from the inventory. After a moment, he looks back up at me, an eyebrow raised.

"What?" I ask.

"You don't have any of your personal items on here."

"Well, I had a bed here. Mattress is gone, but the rest of it is here. Other than that, it's just a little of bourbon and whiskey, but that wasn't stolen. I know who drank that." Trulia Grant.

"Okay, then. I'll take note… I'm afraid this may take a while. Do you have any jobs that were scheduled for today?"

"Yeah, I already called everyone who I had on the books for today and tomorrow. I'll get to the rest some other time, I guess. The only tools I have are some in the car, but it's not enough for most things, mostly an odd number of spares."

"Let's start with your tools. Are all the ones listed here the ones you have?"

"Yeah, I haven't bought any new ones in a while." I dig through my files until I can pull out the most recent receipts I have. "This should cover what I've bought in the past week," I tell Tyler James. "Actually, I may have some in my pocket…" I pull my wallet out and begin going through the receipts in it. "Damn, I think I…"

"Tyson, don't worry too much about it. It seems like just about everything is gone. Do you have insurance?"

"Yeah, but it's not going to cover this much. I'm screwed."

I end up spending most of the day with the police officers and answering questions. The longer it takes, the more I realize all the stuff I had that I don't anymore, from small tools to scraps I could have used for simple repairs, to the stuff for car work.

I don't know what I can even do about it right now. Tomorrow I'll make any necessary phone calls to any jobs I won't be able to do without my tools, and that basically clears any money I was going to make for the next two weeks. And by the way things are looking, I don't think I'll be able to be back in business anytime soon.

I'm so angry at Trulia I can hardly contain it. I can't believe how irresponsible she had been last night, just leaving my warehouse open to be plundered. And now I was ruined. That's what loving gets me, I guess, physical or emotional ruin. Lindsay left me a mess enough, but at least she hadn't taken my livelihood, too.

Before I leave for the day, I make some calls on my cell phone to the scrap yards to see if they have anything I can use. But I soon find there isn't enough scrap metal in this town or the next combined to replace the number of tools that were stolen.

I'm exhausted at this point, so I lock up my empty warehouse and head home, my mind spinning the entire time. I hate this, I hate this, I hate this. If I could go back and never give Trulia access to my warehouse, I would.

Pretty much nothing of hers was taken, and then all of mine was.

When I get home, I flop onto the couch as soon as I enter the living room. My eyes are burning, so I close them for a moment and put my palms over them.

"What are you going to do," I ask myself quietly. "No tools, no scrap, no jobs." I pull the blanket draped over the back of the couch and wrap myself in it, slowly going horizontal until my cheek is pressed into the cushion. Then I turn the television on.

I'm not really paying attention to the sound or even the colors and pictures of the show that's on. I just need something to cling to, a middle distance to focus on.

Trulia Grant has ruined me.

Chapter Twenty-One

As the weeks go by, the girls and I continue to plan the bake sale. Every time I think about all the stuff Tyson lost; I just feel even worse about everything. Whenever I think back to that day, I remember how he even told me to lock the doors behind me as he left.

He lost his whole life because of my mistake. I want to fix this. Hell, I need to fix it, or I won't even be able to return to New York without a heavy heart. After making some calls, I have been able to extend the lease on the sub-let of my apartment. It seems the man there would love to stay another month if possible anyway, so that worked out well for me.

In terms of art, I haven't had much time for that due to the work I've been putting in for the bake sale. Regina and Bridgid have been helping all they can, but their main job is still to take care of our mama's bakery, so most of it is still on me. Not that I mind, though. It was my mistake, so of course it's mine to fix, even if others are willing to step in and help.

I haven't spoken to Tyson since he called me angry and let me know what happened. This isn't to say I haven't tried, though. I call every couple of days and hope he answers, but he never does. It makes me wonder if this is how he felt when I blew up at him.

And to be honest, what he had done was nowhere near as bad as what I had. Now I have two mistakes weighing on me: thinking this was going to be a short-term relationship and getting Tyson's entire warehouse robbed. I know I can't leave until I right both of those wrongs.

Walking into the bakery, I greet Regina who is behind the counter.

"Hey, girl," she says, giving me a hug. "Where have you been? Michael and I didn't see you this morning at breakfast."

"Yeah, that's because I wasn't there. I had to leave early to pick up the fliers." I have designed fliers for the bake sale, and I had so many printed out that there is no way anyone isn't going to know about what we have planned.

"Did you get them distributed today?"

"I got about half. I think I'll do some more tomorrow since it's getting late."

"You know you can hire people to distribute fliers."

"I know, but I'm not trying to add any extra expenses, and it's not as if I have anything else to do. Hopping around town isn't so bad."

"Oh, speaking of that," Reggie says, turning around to the other side of the counter, "the bounce house company called for you earlier. I took a message. I think they wanted to know if you wanted to get snow cones with the deal."

"Hm, that could be nice. Would it take away from the baked goods, though?"

"Possibly. We can talk about it with Bridgid later."

"Definitely." The plan is to rent bounce houses for the kids, asking for donations to enter. And then we want to have fun games that the adults can get in on, too! It's turning out to be a very well-rounded event.

"I can't believe you got Sassafras to come and perform. How much are they?"

"Oh, they said they'll donate their time. Councilman Wilson helped me out with that. And he got the council to approve the square over by the park for the location, so we'll be able to get tons of foot traffic."

"This is all so exciting," Regina says, leaning down and propping her head on her palm. "You really are putting something good together here, Trulia. Good job."

"Thanks, but you know I need to do something big when I'm trying to figure out this mess up."

"Tyson?"

"Yeah. I still feel so bad about the whole thing, Reg. I mean, he even asked me to lock the doors, but I guess I was too drunk to remember it at that point. It's embarrassing."

"What even made you that upset? Were you guys fighting?"

"Yeah, it's weird. Like, we were there to make up— and we had. But I think he was seeing us as this long-term thing, and I had been planning to go back to New York once my sublet was up. He got upset, said I was leading him on. Then he left."

"So I'm sure it didn't help things to have him come the next morning and see everything ruined."

"Exactly. I think he was coming to see if I was there, too, to talk about things. And now he won't talk to me at all."

"When's the last time you called?"

"The day before yesterday. You know I've never done this before. Usually it's me ghosting a person, not the other way around. There's something about him, though. Even if we don't end up dating or anything, I still want to end things right. He's too good, Bridgid."

"What do you mean?"

"Tyson is like the nicest guy I've ever met. Most guys I date are more like James. But Tyson is kind and a gentleman and has these cute freckles that I didn't even know grown men could have but I love. He's amazing. I'm the one who messed up. I should've known he wanted something longer. Then I never would've gotten involved with him just to break his heart."

"I don't know, Trulia. Maybe you want someone like him for the long term. I know it's not how you usually do things and I know it's not your plan, but it could work out maybe."

"Maybe," I sigh. "Well, I should get cleaned up before dinner. Thanks." I give her a hug before leaving. After my shower, I try to reach out to Tyson again with no luck, although I can't blame him. It only makes me that much more determined to raise enough money to get his business functioning again.

I can do this.

Chapter Twenty-Two

TYSON

When I come out of my haze, the world around me is still a little blurry. I blink up at the television. Some show is playing. I think it's reality TV since there's dramatic music playing and head rolls, but I don't know anything else about it, let alone how the show got turned on.

Sighing, I stretch my legs and look around my living room. There are several pizza boxes on the coffee table and trash of chip bags and plastic ware all around. I look back up at the TV and then down at myself. My clothes are stained with grease and have the remnants of the last thing I ate all over them.

I'm not sure if the worst thing about this scene is the trash or the fact that I haven't noticed it until right now.

Hell, I can't even tell you what day it is. Maybe it's also bad that I don't feel the slightest urge to get up and fix any of this… I don't know.

Okay, fine, I've let myself go, but I don't care, and I'm not about to start now. I lift the remote up from where it's lodged in between two cushions and begin changing the channel again. This remote is honestly all I need in the world.

"No, no, no," I say as I flip through the shows. I'm barely even staying on the channels long enough to read the titles or see what the show's about. Half of them are clearly too stimulating, though. I land on the nature channel. Sloths.

I have worked so hard all of my life to have my own business, something I could be proud of. It took a lot of late nights and going without things to even get myself to the point where I was making a profit. Being in a small-town means getting business is even harder than it would be in a big city.

And just because someone has you fix something doesn't mean they'll tell their friends or call you over just to fix it themselves the night before you come. Establishing myself took a long time period of building relationships and a reputation.

Now, I'm not saying that what I had built was an empire by any stretch of the imagination, but it was mine, and it provided more than enough for me to live comfortably on. It also meant I didn't have to work some boring nine to five or be on some guy's crew making minimum wage.

So, no, it wasn't an empire, but it was something big, and to have it all come crashing down at the hands of the sexiest woman I have ever met is… well, crushing to say the least.

The anger isn't as fresh anymore, but the wounds from that day definitely haven't healed much. They're still raw, and here I am pinned to this sofa with nothing but a heavy cloud hanging over me. There's nothing more to do at this point. It's all over.

At first, I had been keeping my phone close to me, but at this point I've left it in a cabinet in the kitchen so that I don't have to deal with it. It's better to just not hear the beeping and vibrations as opposed to having to ignore them.

Sure it means I haven't been talking with Alex much either, but honestly, it's a small price to pay for silence. I'm sure it'll backfire eventually, but it hasn't yet. Of course, I'm saying that just as I hear the lock at my front door clicking.

"Tyson Hayes," Alex sings as he walks into the house. As soon as he crosses the barrier into the living room, his nose scrunches up. "I see you haven't been up to much."

"What's it to you?"

"I mean, maybe it wouldn't be much to me if you answered my phone calls. I had to make sure you were okay."

"I'm fine."

"You don't look fine."

"Relatively."

"Look, I could see why you may be a little down with your warehouse being robbed."

"You mean with my entire livelihood being destroyed all because some girl I wasn't even really dating decided to down a gallon of alcohol and then leave my warehouse unlocked? I don't think I'm exactly overreacting."

"I'm not saying that you are. I'm just saying that this isn't usually how you react to things like this. You're more of a bootstraps sort of guy."

"You realize that's impossible in practice, right? It's just something people say."

"Oh, c'mon, Tyson. Don't be like this."

"How else am I supposed to be, Alex?" I ask.

"Tyson, it smells in here. *You* smell."

I don't answer that, a comment from the nature channel catching my ears. I watch the video, a sloth hanging upside down on a tree. One of its claws swings down to rub its belly. Something about the motion causes me to clutch my own middle, though not scratch it.

"Tyson," Alex says, snapping his fingers at me from across the room. "Focus, dude. You need to get up. You'll be able to think better once you've had a shower and some real food."

"Not. Happening."

"Tyson—"

"Alex, it doesn't matter how many times you say my name or the tone you say it in. I'm not moving from here. There's no reason to, and you know it."

"Look, I get it. The whole world came crashing down. I'm not denying that. But I am denying your right to just let it stay like that. You need to figure out what you're going to do next the same way you always do. This isn't the first time you've had problems."

"No, I just... No, Alex. This isn't like all of the other times. I've never had to start from scratch before, I've never not been able to work. I've never been betrayed like this."

Sighing, Alex comes further into the house and takes a seat on the arm of the couch, crossing his arms. Looks like he's not going to be leaving anytime soon, but I'm not either.

Chapter Twenty-Three

TRULIA

"Are you ready?" Bridgid asks me. We're standing at the entrance to our big bake sale right before it's supposed to open. The energy of the square is buzzing. All of the vendors are ready. We've dotted every 'i' and crossed every 't' and see a line of people already collecting behind the donation tables.

"So ready," I answer. "It's amazing, isn't it? I couldn't have imagined it coming out this well, but the turnout is already climbing, and we haven't even opened yet. I'm proud." I chuckle.

"You should be Trulia. I mean, sure we helped, but all of this was your brain, child."

"No, don't say that. You and Regina have put a lot into helping me. So have so many other people. If it weren't for that, none of this would've been made possible. I really think we may be able to make enough to get Tyson his tools back."

"Hopefully. And if not, you're at least going to help with a chunk of the expenses."

"I guess, but I really want to get it all now. I don't know what I'll do if it's not enough."

"Oh, stop thinking like that. Come on, we should take our places." Bridgid drags me over to our booth, and we take a seat at the table with our money box.

"Good morning," I say to the Anderson family, who's taken a spot at the front of the line at our column for the bake sale. "Thank you all for coming. I really appreciate it."

"Of course," Mrs. Anderson says. "It's for a good cause. We all love Tyson Hayes. And besides, it's a beautiful Saturday. It'd be a shame to spend it inside, don't you think?" Mrs. Anderson pulls a wad of cash for her donation out of her purse and hands it to me.

"Well, you're right about that. Thank you. You all can go ahead inside. The bake sale is on the perimeter— we have those cake pops you and the girls love— and then behind that you'll find the bounce houses and band."

"Perfect, you have a good one." The family proceeds inside.

It's so great to see everyone coming to support the bake sale. When someone in the town is in need, all of the people seem to really pull together to help, a brand of unity I find myself having missed after being away in New York for so long.

It's not that I don't have an artist community in New York, but it's just so different from being around my sisters and all these people I grew up with. I'm going to hate to have to go back. If anything, this bake sale is also a sign that I need to come back and visit more.

As I take people's donations and organize them in the money box, I can't help but think of Tyson, of putting these crisp bills in his hands. Even if he never wants to see me again, I know I have to make right by him. What happened is all my fault, so he shouldn't have to suffer for it.

Since things happened, no one I've talked to has seen him around. Sometimes I wonder if he's hiding from me, but I also don't think he even knows I'm still in town, so that's not likely. I wish I could talk to him, let him know that I'm trying to fix things and just how sorry I am. But he hasn't answered my calls, not even once.

Despite my sadness at how everything has turned out between me and Tyson, I'm able to keep a smile on my face as people pour in and enjoy the event we put together. By the end of the day, Bridgid, Regina, and I are bone tired. We still have a little more to absorb for the bounce house rentals and everything, but if the other boxes are anything like mine, I'm sure we'll have enough money to give to Tyson in the end.

We're grateful for the men in the community who volunteered to handle the breakdown so that we could leave and get back to the bakery sooner. Once we have all the surfaces cleaned off, we head back to the bakery with the money boxes to count our earnings.

"What an amazing event!" Regina says as we lock the bakery door behind us and take a seat at one of the tables. "It seems like everyone had fun, and by the looks of my box, I think we made a lot."

"Yeah, I think so, too," Bridgid says. "Trulia and I got a lot at our table, too. Even though I'm tired, I had so much fun. I love watching the little ones eat their cake pops and cookies. It's the cutest thing."

"How about you, Trulia?" Regina asks as they both turn to me, quieter than usual.

"Um, yeah. I'm happy with it," I say, already opening one of the boxes to count the money. It has been a great day, but I still want to see how much we have. I'm hoping it's enough for Tyson, but I know I can't really be happy until I see how much we got.

"It's enough, Trulia."

"Let's just count."

Chuckling, they each take stacks and begin counting the money with me, each of us carefully tallying whenever we reach one hundred. Once we've all counted separately, I take the calculator and add everything up together. When I see the number, I feel tears pooling in my eyes. I slide the calculator over to show the girls. We've made just over two thousand dollars.

"Wow," Regina says, her smile growing. "We did good, girls!"

"So good!" I say, beaming. "I can't wait to give this to Tyson. I just know he'll be excited, too. I can't believe we did this. Thank you!" I stand to give both of my sisters a hug, knowing I couldn't have done this without them.

Tomorrow can't come fast enough.

Chapter Twenty-Four

Tyson

"Oh, come on, Ty. We've been here for half an hour, and you still haven't moved," Alex says to me. He's not seated on the arm of the couch anymore and is instead leaning against the wall behind it with a frown.

"I already told you I'm not moving, Alex, doing just as I said I'd do."

"Dude get up! I get that you're sad about what happened, but the least you can do is get a shower or something. None of this is a reason to just totally give up on life and sit there forever. You need to clean yourself up, then this mess, and then figure out what you want to do next."

"And what's that next supposed to be?"

"I don't know. Maybe I'll help you think through it if you just get a shower or something. It isn't like you to just sit here and not do anything. You're not one of those guys who fails and then just gives up, Tyson, so I don't know why you're acting like it."

Sighing, I'll admit that this funk is definitely one of the deeper (if not the deepest) ones I've been in. I don't know why this setback is hitting me like it is, just that it is. Sitting up, I hunch over my lap for a moment. What am I doing?

"Get. Up."

"I know, I know," I say finally, scratching my head.

"Shower, Tyson. I'm going to start in here."

"Give me a minute, I'm going." Defeatedly, I leave the couch and walk off into the hallway to get a shower. Usually I enjoy these, but this one's all business. I soap up, rinse off, and manage to wash my hair in about five minutes.

Once I finish that, I consider shaving, but I don't have the energy to do it, so I just jump into some clothes and throw my crusty old ones into the hamper. I know I should feel better after cleaning up a bit, but I don't.

I stare at myself in the mirror. I haven't been doing much, but I still haven't been sleeping much, so there are these dark smudges under my eyes. The corners of my mouth are turned down. My face is still red from the steam of the water.

It's not that I don't recognize myself— I do. It's just that I feel outside of me, as if a ghost of me is standing to the side with a pitying expression. I break my gaze away from the mirror.

When I walk back out, I see Alex tackling the giant mess in the living room, right now scrubbing some stain on the carpet that's proving tough. It's then that I feel this wave of embarrassment wash over me, burning my cheeks and my chest.

Looking at my life with clean eyes, I'm ashamed of how I just let myself go. Alex is right. It's not like me to just give in so easily. I'm usually more resilient. When challenges come, I just adapt. I don't hide. At least, I didn't used to hide.

"I'm sorry, Alex," I say, stepping up to help get the rest of the house clean. I collect the dishes from the coffee table and begin loading them into the dishwasher. Alex comes behind me with a trash bag.

"Don't be sorry, Tyson. You know I don't mind like that. The only mistake you made was not answering my calls for over a week…" Even though I was annoyed to see Alex when he first arrived, I'm beginning to be a little grateful that he came to help me out of this trench. I can't wallow in the mud forever, can I?

"I shouldn't be doing this."

"You'll figure it out." At this point, we've finished cleaning up the mess. Most of it was just the living room, anyway. Alex and I move to take a seat at the kitchen table. It's as if he thinks I'll be glued to the couch again if I sit there so soon.

"I don't know," I say, propping my head on my palm. I really don't know. I don't know what to say, what to do, how to move forward from this. I'm stuck.

"You should come out into town with me. We can walk around, get an ice cream cone or a sandwich. Getting out would be good."

"No, I'm not getting out. I'm fine here."

"You can't stay inside forever. I think it's better you just rip the band aid off, you know? What's it going to help sitting in here longer, Tyson?"

"I'm not saying it's going to help. I mean, it's not. But still, I can't yet. Maybe another day." I meet his eyes with a sad smile. I wonder if he can tell my mind's focused on other things.

"What is it?" Alex asks.

"The truth is… Even with all Trulia did, I still think about her. And not just bad things. Like, despite having all of my tools stolen by her thoughtlessness, I still miss her. Even when I was ignoring her calls, I was thinking about her, about how much fun I had. The night everything happened, we were supposed to be starting over. We'd gotten in an argument, but I'd come back the next day so that we could make it right. That's when I saw how she'd left everything open for the robber."

"I mean, it makes sense to miss her. You can miss somebody and still hate something they did. Can I tell you something? You have to promise to not get mad."

"What?"

"I remember how you were a year ago. I mean, Lindsay really did a number on you. You were like a shell of yourself forever, and then you had kind of recovered but not quite. When you were with Trulia, it seemed like you'd finally come back into yourself again. But how you are now isn't that far from how you were then. I think she made you better."

"I don't even know where she is in New York. Besides, she's probably moved so far beyond me. I wasn't her type anyway."

"I don't know…"

Even if Alex doesn't think so, I know it's over.

Chapter Twenty-Five

My heart hammers against my rib cage, and I want nothing more than to turn around and walk away. Nerves. I've never understood how people avoided doing a task because they were nervous until now.

My stance has always been to be sure of myself, in everything I do.

There have never been nerves. I've never been anxious in my life, and the fact that it was creeping up while I'm on my way to see Tyson was more unnerving than anything.

Well, it was more *annoying* than anything. Because now isn't the time for nerves.

I always know what's happening around me, I always know what I want. But, with Tyson, it seems like I'm always doing the wrong thing. I'm one step behind, or I misread the situation. He throws me off guard, unlike anyone else I've ever met.

Maybe that's why I'm so nervous.

And that bothers me. I never let anyone catch me off guard.

I sigh and walk up the stairs to Tyson's door.

I don't want to talk. I'd rather hide from him than talk. I still feel guilty for what I did to him, for leaving his warehouse open. This envelope of cash weighs heavy in my hands. A lot of people had gone to a lot of work to make this cash for Tyson, showing how loved he really is in this town. I know I need to suck it up.

And I need to swallow my pride and confront him.

Even though I know I hurt him deeply.

So, I walk up to his door, and knock a few times. Then, I wait. And I wait. And I wait. I brush my hair out of my eyes, just needing something to do with my hands.

What if he doesn't answer? What if he leaves you standing outside his door?

The thought just hit me, and the nerves double in my chest as I think about it.

What if he doesn't answer me? What the hell am I supposed to do with $2,000 of fundraiser money?

I brush my hair out of my face again, then look at the door. Should I knock again? I'm not sure what the proper etiquette is for knocking on the door of a man whose heart I've broken.

Then, the handle jiggles, and the fear in my heart skyrockets.

Suddenly, I desperately want him not to be home. Maybe it's a friend I can give the money to.

The envelope nearly slips from my hands by the sudden onset of fear. I have to control my breathing, to focus.

"Hold on!" I hear Tyson call through the door.

He's home.

Shit.

Suddenly I'd rather be anywhere but on this doorstep right now. I'd rather be anywhere but here.

The door swings open, and I'm faced with the man who leaves me breathless.

"H-Hey," I stammer. He looks me up and down, as if I'm a ghost. As if he'd never seen me in my life and was more surprised than anything to see me on his doorstep. Granted, our last conversation didn't go well, so I'm not sure what I've been expecting.

But the complete and utter shock across his face wasn't it. Before he slams the door in my face, I need to say something. I need to say something, anything, to break the silence between us.

"Can I talk to you for a second?" I ask, keeping the desperation out of my voice. The plea seeps through. I need him to listen to me, need him to listen to what I have to say.

"Yeah," he says, then, he steps back in the door awkwardly. I walk past him, noticing the newly tidied up house.

Suddenly, it hits me that maybe he was in the middle of something. Maybe he didn't care about our last encounter at all.

That makes me feel worse. I blush and try to keep myself together.

"Nice place," I say, trying to break the awkwardness between us. It doesn't work, and Tyson gives me a weird smile. Then, he leads me to the couch in the living room.

We sit an awkward distance away from each other, and I stare at him, flattening my skirt. I almost forget why I'm here, I'm just so happy to see him. Even if his face is utterly confused, I'm still happy to see him.

I find myself hoping that I didn't interrupt something.

I open my mouth to say something at the same time that he does. And we both laugh, shrug, and look away.

I'm not blind to how ridiculous this is. We're adults, not teenagers. This is a business transaction to alleviate the strain of a robbery.

"Sorry," he says. "You go first."

"No, I think it's fair that you go first," I answer, needing a minute to collect myself.

"I thought you were in New York," he stammers. "You said you were going to be leaving after the month, and I thought that's where you'd be…"

"No, no."

I find myself talking fast, which is odd for me. I'm not thinking about my words, I just want him to listen to me. I just want him to listen to me before he throws me out of his apartment.

"I couldn't leave, not after what I did to you. I'm just so sorry, Tyson. I didn't mean... you know I would never…"

I breathe deeply, stopping myself. He does not need to hear this from me, not right now.

"Here," I shove the envelope into his hands. "We did some work... we had a fundraiser. My sisters did a ton of work, most of it…" I shrug. "And a lot of people helped. This town really loves you."

His eyes go wide as he looks inside the envelope.

"Seriously, it was nothing, I just couldn't leave without making it right. Now, you can probably buy new tools or whatever you need..."

I want to stay, I definitely want to stay, but I also want to get away from this situation as fast as possible. I don't know what to do, or what I want. Which, to me, is more uncomfortable than the awkward situation.

So, I stare at him, as he looks at the cash in the envelope. Completely stunned into silence.

And I wait.

It's all I can do.

Chapter Twenty-Six

TYSON

I'm sitting across from Trulia, who is more nervous than I have ever seen anyone in my life. Just when I think this encounter can't get any more awkward, she hands me an envelope of cash, stating that she raised the money to pay off the tools I lost due to the robbery.

I'm speechless. I have no idea how to respond to this—how does one respond to this? I sit there, not moving a muscle, just staring at the envelope in my hand for a while.

A million thoughts are running through my mind right now. Not only did Trulia stay in town when I thought she was gone this whole time—but she stayed because of *me*. The last time we spoke, I was insanely mad at her and frankly, quite rude—and yet she stayed here for me, even when she was supposed to be back in New York now.

What am I supposed to do with that information? Is it supposed to make me happy? Because right now, it's just confusing me. If she was here all this time, how come she didn't say something to me earlier? Why did she wait so long?

I refocus my eyes on the envelope. She waited because she wanted to give me this money. No one has ever done something like this for me before. No one has ever helped me like this. I don't even know what to say.

All I know is that I have to forgive her now. She has clearly been through enough guilt since the robbery, and the amount of money in this envelope has made her mistake more than ameliorative. Finally, I look up at her.

"I forgive you, Trulia," I state, getting up and sitting right next to her.

She lets out a sigh of relief.

"Thank you, Tyson, thank you so much. Is there any way at all that we could just start over? Is there any way that we could be friends?" She begs.

"Ha-ha, you're silly."

Trulia's face falls, and I realize how that must have sounded.

"No—no… what I meant is that I could never be *just* friends with you Tru…"

Without waiting for a response, I pull her into a kiss. The feel of her lips on mine again after our time apart—it feels more perfect than I ever could have imagined. Scoping her up off the couch and into my arms, I realize that I simply can't resist this woman. We share kisses all the way to my bedroom, where I toss her onto my bed.

We simultaneously rip our clothes off, tossing them out of sight, before coming together, molding into one. She lies on her back and I rest her ankles up on my shoulders. The moment I enter her, my entire world falls back into place.

I pound into her, forgetting about everything else around me. Starting off slow and rhythmic, I gradually increase my speed. Our sex this time around feels more intimate. Less desperate. It feels like love.

As I get closer to my climax, that desperation comes back, and my pace quickens. As we come together, we stare into each other's eyes, and neither of us has to say how we're feeling out loud, we already know.

I collapse beside her, catching my breath before round two. Once Trulia has come down from her high, she turns to me and props herself up on her elbow. We lock eyes, as she trails her fingers up and down my chest, across my stomach, across my groin and back up again.

She pulls herself up onto me and begins kissing every inch of my body.

I close my eyes, enjoying the feeling of her soft lips caressing my skin. No woman has ever taken the time to make me feel like this. No woman has ever shown me this much attention during sex before. It's nice to be with someone who wants to please you as much as you want to please them.

"I'm gonna ride you now," Tru whispers in my ear, reaching down and stroking my cock. She continues to stroke me as she gets up into a sitting position above me. She grabs my legs and positions them so that my knees are up behind her and my feet are flat on the bed, before slowly lowering herself onto my cock.

Hooking her arms around and through the backs of my knees, she begins to ride me. This girl never ceases to amaze me. After she gets used to me, she goes wild, hopping up and down on my dick.

I never even knew I could be this loud, but Trulia brings it out in me. I groan as she fucks me, watching her breasts bouncing along with her. Each time she goes back down, she tightens her pussy, giving me that extra amount of pleasure. I can't take it anymore.

I grab her hips and work mine with hers. I slam up into her, our hips perfectly synchronized. I can tell she's about to come as she lets go of all control, tightens her grip on my legs and leans her neck back, mouth wide open. That's when I use everything left in me to go even faster, until the sound of our skin slapping together drowns out everything else.

The two of us come together for the second time, our bodies still working together until we reach the peak of our climax. She lifts herself off of me and collapses onto my chest, wrapping her body around mine.

We cuddle into each other, completely entangled, as we slowly fall into a deep sleep…

Chapter Twenty-Seven

TRULIA

My eyes flutter open and I roll over lazily, check the time, and then snuggle back in with Tyson. It seems that we accidentally fell asleep and took a three-hour nap—it's almost dark outside.

I can tell that Tyson is still fast asleep from his little snore. Usually snoring drives me crazy, but Tyson's is quiet and actually quite adorable. I could definitely get used to this. The only question is—do I want to?

I was doing great in New York City focusing on my career, not letting boys or anything get in the way of becoming a great artist. I loved it that way, and I'm not sure if I'd be willing to let all of that go to keep Tyson around. And Tyson definitely does *not* seem like the kind of guy who would pick up his life and move to the city, especially with how attached he is to his family.

When I think about going back to New York, I feel relief. Relief that I'll be going back to the place that I love so dearly. The crazy people that I love, the career I love—all of that. But then I also think about leaving my sisters behind again. And now that Regina is staying here—I'm not sure if I'm ready to do that.

This would be the first chance since we were all teens that we would all be living in the same place at the same time. This would be my chance to reconnect with my family again. And then there's Mama. I know for a fact that Mama would be so genuinely happy to see the three of us together again. But Mama would also want me to be happy, and if she knew this place didn't make me happy—then she wouldn't want me to be forced to stay.

The truth is, I'm not actually sure *what* would make me happy right now. I mean, with Tyson in my life—Belton feels different. It feels like a town that I would actually want to stay and live the rest of my life in. It's just hard for me to imagine myself doing that after so many years of telling myself I never would.

I spent at least the last ten years thinking that New York City would be my forever home. I never thought even for a second that I would come back here. I mean, what about my art? How would I build a career here? New York was the perfect place for me to express my artistic self. In Belton, well—I've just never really been able to do that here.

I go over it and over it in my head as I listen to Tyson's soft snores, until suddenly they stop, and Tyson wraps his arm tightly around me, kissing the top of my head. I close my eyes, and right in this moment, I am perfectly happy, and all my dilemmas fade away.

"You're amazing," I whisper, before angling myself towards him and sharing a kiss.

"You should stay," he whispers back.

I shoot right up into a sitting position.

"Huh?"

"I said, you should stay," he repeats, sitting up next to me.

"Umm-"

"Hear me out... you could stay here and stay with me and just work on your art project. It's going to take a while longer anyway, so why not? I know you don't want to go back to New York yet, because if you did then you already would have."

Before I can respond, he continues.

"I know I sound crazy, and maybe I am... but think about it. It would be perfect. I could help you with your sculpture. Trulia, your tree sculpture is already turning out *amazing,* you can't give up on it. You have to finish it. And when that's done—I could help you work on all sorts of other things. I could teach you things, you could teach me things. How many offers do you get like this in New York?"

Finally, he seems to run out of words, and I stare at him, dumbfounded—shocked. Is he really asking me what I think he's asking? He wants me to forego my place in New York and move in with him? I mean—that would be crazy, right? There's just no way he's serious about this. But from the look in his eyes—I can tell that he really is serious.

I open my mouth to speak, but nothing comes out. I don't know what to say, or how I'm supposed to react. Luckily, he doesn't wait for me to. He leans over and plants a big kiss on my lips. When he pulls away, he gives me such a warm smile that I almost blurt out yes.

"Just think about," he says, before hopping out of bed and throwing on a robe. "You want some dinner?"

"Yes *please,* I'm starved!" I shout, jumping out of bed with him.

I throw on one of his oversized white t-shirts, and we make our way into the kitchen.

"I remember you saying you aren't much of a cook, so I'll make everything. All you have to do is sit there and look beautiful."

"Good, because I was *not* about to help you. What's on tonight's menu?"

"Steak, macaroni and cheese, green beans, and some buttery rolls. How does that sound?"

"You know how to make all of that? From scratch? And it turns out good?"

The baffled look on my face causes him to burst out laughing, making my cheeks burn in embarrassment.

"Oh you're so cute. Yes, I know how to make all of that, from scratch. And it'll taste better than good."

"It's just—I've never had a man cook for me before—this is completely new territory for me."

"Well then your mind is about to be *blown*."

Over the next hour and a half, Tyson cooks while I dance around him to some very loud Fleetwood Mac, serving him kisses while he serves me little tastes of the food he's making.

The meal turns out to be *amazing*—possibly even better than Reggie's, although I would never dare to say that to her face. We spend the rest of the night eating, and we even end up going one more round in the bedroom before we fall asleep next to each other again. At least, *he* falls asleep. I spend most of the night listening to his snores and thinking about the offer he presented me, wondering if I should take it.

Chapter Twenty-Eight

A week has now gone by since the first night that Trulia spent the night at my house. She has spent the night every single night since then. It's also been a week since I asked her to stay in Belton with me. She never responded, and neither of us has brought it up since.

Things have been going so well between us that I don't want to risk bringing it up and disrupting our peace. Besides, I suspect that her staying over for the past week kind of *is* an answer, whether she realizes that or not.

I know it sounds crazy, me asking this girl to move in with me after practically just meeting her. Maybe I sound like I'm obsessed with her or something. But I truly just have this feeling that this is what is supposed to be. Whenever

I'm around her, everything just feels… *right*. And I can't ignore that feeling.

The way I feel for Trulia, is unlike anything I've ever experienced before. I *never* felt like this with Lindsay—never. Tru gives me this thrill, like I'm excited to live life for the first time. She makes me excited to get up every morning. She makes me excited to go to sleep at night so that I can wake up the next day and see her. And of course—the sex is *amazing*. Beyond amazing.

Every day, I wake up at my usual time, *way* before her—and go out for my run. By the time I get back and shower, she still isn't awake, so I prepare her an omelet. The smell of food usually wakes her up by the time I'm done, and she slips into the kitchen to enjoy some breakfast with me.

After breakfast, she heads over to the warehouse while I set out to do some jobs, and when I'm done with my jobs, I bring her a late lunch. Then I'll spend some time helping her with her project, and we go home and eat some dinner.

I have to keep reminding myself that I can't get *too* attached to this routine of ours, because I still don't know if she's staying. Plus, it's not like we're in an official relationship. Even if she does stay—there's no telling if she'll want to actually be with me long-term.

Regardless of all the what-ifs, I'm happy. I don't care about the uncertainty of it all, because even if she does leave—at least I'll have had this time with her. She's practically moved in with me, and I *still* can't get enough of her.

With the money from the fundraiser Trulia and her sisters put together, I was able to buy all brand-new tools replacing every last one that was stolen from me. I've never even owned brand-new tools before, all of mine were old janky hand-me-downs. I couldn't be more thankful for Tru and her sisters for doing that for me. I'm beginning to think the robbery might have been a blessing in disguise. I think it brought the two of us closer in some weird way.

I even had a little extra money after buying my new tools, and Trulia suggested I should outfit my truck so that it would be easier for me to do jobs. Speaking of jobs, with my new tools I'm able to do so much more work that I couldn't do with my old ones, so I've been completely flooded with tons of jobs. I've been doing lots of work for people around town, so much that I'm even considering hiring someone to help me.

Today I got done pretty late and left Trulia a message that I was too tired and would just meet her at the house today whenever she was done. I wasn't expecting her to arrive for another two hours, so I'm surprised when I hear the front door opening, signaling that she's home. A huge smile spreads across my face as I head to meet her.

"Hey what are you doing home so early?"

"Well, you left me a message saying how tired you were, and so I figured I would take the rest of the day off of my project and come pamper you. I brought you some burgers, fries, and rib tips—your favorite takeout!" She explains, holding up a bunch of takeout bags.

"Oh my—Tru you did not have to do this; this is so nice!"

"Well, I figured you wouldn't want to cook since you're so tired and I sure as hell wasn't going to cook—how else were we going to eat tonight?"

"I suppose you're right," I say, taking some of the bags from her and setting them on the coffee table.

"So what do you say we eat in front of the television and watch movies together all night—I'll even let you pick which ones."

"I think that's a great idea Tru, but first-"

I pull her into my arms and kiss her long and hard. Every day when I leave to go do my jobs, and she goes to the warehouse—I dream of the moment I'll get to kiss her again. She hops into my arms, wrapping her legs around my waist, and kisses me back.

We spend the rest of the night huddled up on the couch, smashing our faces and sneaking kisses here and there. I watch her sometimes, while she's watching the TV, and I find myself getting a bit emotional.

I don't want to live without this girl. She makes me so unbelievably happy with barely any effort. Trulia has made me feel more in the month or so that I've known her than any woman, even my ex-wife, has ever made me feel. I don't want to ever lose that, but I still don't know how long Trulia will be sticking around for…

Chapter Twenty-Nine

TRULIA

It's been a few days since Tyson asked me to stay in Belton with him. I haven't given him an answer yet, and neither of us have brought it up since. To be honest, the whole thing kind of shocked me.

Don't get me wrong—I love spending time with Ty. We always have so much fun, and he motivates me—like truly motivates me. He makes me see more in myself that I never saw before. He makes me believe that my art really is worth all the blood, sweat, and tears.

I love our daily routine together; I love how he always makes sure I've eaten enough. I love how much he cares—it's really hard to come by anyone who really and truly cares. I mean you meet people all the time who say they care, and they say they'll do all types of things—but when it really comes down to it, it's themselves that they care about. Most people don't really give two shits about you at the end of the day. It's sad, but it's true.

That's not the case with Tyson. Tyson seems to care more about me than he does himself. Since the very day we met, he has always put my needs and wants before his own. It makes me feel special and deserving. He cares in a way that doesn't make me feel like I owe him anything back.

Despite all of that—we haven't known each other for that long. New York is my life, how am I just supposed to agree to put my life on hold for someone I only just met?

Only the more I think about it, the less it feels like putting my life on hold and the more it feels like my life is finally starting. I just want to make sure that I'm making the right decision before my impulses take over.

I just can't help but shake this feeling that despite why I originally came back to Belton (Mama), there was another reason that I was supposed to come here. And maybe that reason is Tyson. So until I figure that out, I know in my heart that I can't leave.

The two of us had an amazing night together yesterday. I came home early and surprised him with some takeout. We spent all night together, and I couldn't ignore the fact that last night together made me feel like this was where I belonged, with him. But for some reason, that scares the shit out of me.

If I'm being completely honest, I've never really felt like this before with anyone. I've never met someone who just felt like home. Someone I felt completely comfortable around, someone I trusted with every ounce of my being.

Feeling all of these things, it's just scary especially when you've never felt them before. I'm not exactly sure how to navigate this, and I don't want to hurt Tyson while I'm trying to figure that out.

I take a break from my project to get up and stretch. I haven't been able to get much done today, my mind is running a mile a minute. Usually I'm able to put whatever I'm thinking about aside and just focus on my art, but today I just can't stop thinking about Tyson's proposition. I know I need to give him an answer soon, and so it's been weighing on me a little extra.

Right on schedule, Tyson's truck pulls up outside. The moment he walks in, our eyes lock and his face lights up. Something about that smile of his turns my insides into jelly every time I see it.

He meets me halfway and sweeps me into his arms and immediately pulls me into a deep kiss. His lips are so familiar to me now, I know every inch of them. When he pulls away, I'm gasping, and I find myself clutching onto him for support.

"Well hello to you too," I joke.

"Oh I'm sorry, was that not a proper greeting?"

"No, it was a perfect greeting," I smile, pecking him on the lips.

He smiles back at me, and I look into his eyes, wondering if this is how wonderful life could be every day if I were to make the commitment to stay here. Quickly pushing that thought to the side, I reach up and hook my hand behind his neck, pulling him back in for another kiss.

We kiss for a long while until we're interrupted by the growl coming from my stomach. The two of us giggle while pulling away.

"You didn't eat today? I leave early for one morning and you can't even make yourself some cereal? Come on, girl —what would you do without me, starve?"

"Probably, so what's for dinner Chef Hayes?"

"Follow me home and find out, missy."

"Noo, tell me now—what if I don't like it?"

"Ugh fine, I'm making cajun chicken breast with some herb potatoes and veggies. Since when are you picky?"

"Since you made that disgusting white cheddar pasta last week!"

"Who doesn't like white cheddar??"

"Me!!"

"Okay well I'll make sure to take note of that in my Trulia notebook," he says, rolling his eyes.

"Smart ass," I mumble as I turn away to grab my purse.

"Hey! I heard that!" He laughs, smacking my ass.

The two of us engage in a wrestling match that lasts until we almost crash into my sculpture. We collapse onto the floor, catching our breath before heading home to start dinner.

Chapter Thirty

Tyson

I wake up from an amazing dream. One of those dreams that you never want to end, and you can't help but feel a little sad when they do. But the sadness goes away instantly when I open my eyes and see the woman cuddled up against my bare chest.

I stare at her as she sleeps, admiring her beauty. She looks so peaceful, like an angel when she's sleeping. She doesn't make any noise, and she barely moves at all the entire night. Just one more thing to make me fall even more for this girl.

As I admire her, I wonder how on earth I ever could have compared her to Lindsay. This woman is nothing like Lindsay, not even a little bit. I feel bad for ever thinking she could have been. The more I watch her, the more I realize that I'm not just falling for her… I'm already in love with her.

I'm in love with Trulia. The more I think about it, the more I know that it's true. I love this girl in a way that I've never loved *anyone,* including Lindsay. I love this girl and I can't let her leave Belton without telling her that. I have to try to get her to stay, because I know this is something she wants, she's just too scared to take that leap. I have to show her that she doesn't need to be scared.

The only thing I can think of is to ask her sisters for some help. They know her better than anyone, and they'll know exactly what I should do in this situation. Maybe they can even talk some sense into her. I decide to go have a little visit with them tomorrow after Tru goes to the warehouse.

As for today, I think it's about time I hijack our workday and steal Trulia away for a little date. Slithering out of bed while trying not to wake her in the process, I tiptoe out of the room and into the kitchen. I decide to take her to one of my favorite spots to go and enjoy the hot weather, and that's Belton Lake, only about a ten-minute drive from my house.

I dig out an old picnic basket that I keep for days like this and pack it full of everything I can find that we might like. Strawberries, bananas, cheese, some BLT sandwiches with ham, some bottled water, and I even throw in a wine bottle and two glasses. I round up a giant blanket for us to lay on, and then hide the supplies in the back of my truck so my surprise isn't ruined.

A few minutes later, Trulia rolls out of bed and comes to find me. Perfect timing.

"You're up a little early this morning, you know I don't like waking up without you next to me," she says with a pout, throwing her arms around me.

"Well, I think I have something that will make up for that."

"Oh yeah? What could that possibly be?"

"I'm kidnapping you today and taking you somewhere special. No working today, only fun. How does that sound?"

"Hmm, well normally I hate being told what to do—but I actually think I'm okay with this. I need a break from the warehouse anyway. Where are we going??"

"It's a surprise," I reply with a smirk.

"Oh come onnn just tell me," she whines.

"Nope! Go ahead and get ready, so we can get on the road."

"Oh so it's far away?"

"I didn't say that," I say with a wink, smacking her ass as she walks out of the room.

"Can you at least tell me what I should wear?"

"Hmm, something you'll be comfortable in outdoors."

She narrows her eyes at me as she leaves to get ready, and I can't help but laugh. Today is going to be a good day, I just know it.

Twenty minutes later, Trulia emerges from our room wearing a bright yellow sundress that stops just above her knees, and those bright white sneakers she loves so much. Her lips are bright red, and her hair is tied back into a long braid that goes past her waist. Even though I see her every single day, I'm still breathless just looking at her. How did I ever get this lucky?

We head out without breakfast; I tell her we'll have plenty of food to eat when we get there. She seems to have forfeited because she doesn't even comment on that.

I take a few detours so that the ride seems longer than it is, just to tease her. When we get there, I park the car and hop out, fishing the picnic basket and the blanket out of the back of the truck.

"Oh my god… are we having a picnic on the water??" She exclaims.

"That we are!"

"Oh my goodness I've never done this before, this is like my dream date!"

I take her hand and lead us to a good spot by the water, surrounded by trees and beautiful yellow flowers. We spread out the blanket and collapse onto it next to each other.

We're silent for a moment, staring up at the sky, watching the branches above us waving back and forth in the wind. It's the perfect day, for the perfect date, and my heart feels unbelievably full.

"Okay I'm starving now, what do we have?"

We unload the basket, spreading everything out around us buffet style. Seeing Trulia beaming and enjoying herself on such a simple date, just confirms that she really is my person. We were meant to be together, and there's no way I can lose her. She's mine.

After we feast on most of the food, and down the bottle of wine together, we snuggle up on our blanket as she traces lines into my skin. Suddenly she jumps up.

"I have an idea!! Get up, come on!"

Needing no convincing, I follow her. She runs to the shore of the lake and begins lifting her dress over her head.

"Whoa, Tru what are you doing?"

"Relax, I wore a bra today. We're going swimming!"

"We are?"

"Yes!" She says, lifting my shirt over my head.

Once we're both in our underwear, she takes my hand and leads us into the water. The lake is warm today, it takes no time at all for us to get used to the temperature.

"This was an amazing idea, Tru, I'm shocked at you."

Trulia turns to me and smiles, the sun shining down on her hazel eyes, making them appear even brighter. She wades towards me and pulls me in for a kiss, hoisting herself up and wrapping her arms and legs around me. She looks around us in awe.

"Isn't this the most felicitous view you've ever seen?" she marvels.

"Stunning," I agree. But I'm not looking at the view, I'm looking at her.

Chapter Thirty-One

TRULIA

Waking up in Tyson's arms has now become my absolute favorite thing. If it were up to me, I would never leave this bed where I'm safely snuggled up to his muscular body.

Yesterday turned out to be the most amazing day. Tyson took me to Lake Belton to have a little picnic. I'd been to that lake a thousand times during my childhood, but until yesterday I had no idea how beautiful it could be.

The two of us enjoyed a picnic by the water, and then we went swimming until our skin turned all wrinkled and pruney. After that, we were so exhausted that we ended up napping together on the blanket he brought. We woke up about two hours later, and he took us to dinner at a nice, fancy Italian restaurant.

Sure, Tyson and I have spent practically every day together since we met. But yesterday was the first time we actually went on what you might call a real date. It was so nice to spend time together when neither of us were working. Of course, we send time together at home every single day—but making the time to go out together is different.

All day I just kept thinking—is this what life with him would be like? Is this what it would be like if I stayed and officially moved in with him? Because if I'm being completely honest with myself—I would be okay with that. A life with Tyson is definitely a life I would want for myself, and better than I could've dreamed my life would end up.

He feels like home. No man has ever felt like home to me before. In fact, all of this is totally new territory for me. He makes me feel wanted, needed, important. As cheesy as it sounds, he really does make me feel like I'm the only girl in the world. And who doesn't want to feel like that?

I keep waiting for this feeling to go away, but honestly it just gets stronger each day. I'm not really sure what to make of that, but I've got more important things to worry about right now—like my sculpture.

I was more than happy to take yesterday off from working on it, but now it's back to business. It's almost completely done, but for the past week I've just been feeling like it's missing something.

I've been scouring my brain for what needs to be finished, but nothing comes up. Usually when a project of mine is close to being finished, I always find one little detail about it that isn't exactly right. But I've never been in a position where I wasn't even sure what was wrong with it. I just can't seem to put my finger on it this time.

As Tyson and I get ready for the day, I continue to think about what my sculpture could possibly be missing. I shovel down some waffles, and then put on some coffee for us.

"You're in quite a hurry this morning!" Tyson notes.

"Hey, gotta make up for the time I lost yesterday because of *someone*," I tease him.

He scoops me up into his arms, runs into our room and throws me onto the bed, tickling me as I burst into laughter.

"Hey! What's my one rule!" I shout between laughs.

"No tickling…" he admits, letting me go.

"So what do you owe me?"

"A massage…"

"A *full body* massage," I correct him.

"Fine, fine," he says as he plants kisses all over my neck.

"I'll be sure to collect later on tonight, mister."

He continues to kiss my neck, creating a trail from my collarbone to my ear. Finally, he reaches me lips. He kisses me softly, like I could break into pieces at any sudden movement, until the kiss becomes more urgent, like I'm going off to war and this is the last one we'll ever share.

Completely forgetting about my plans for the day, I surrender myself to him, matching his urgency. I wrap my legs around him, pulling him closer to me. You would think after all the sex we had last night that both of us would be beyond tired, but it's pretty clear that we're both hungry for more.

That is, until I come back down to earth and slowly break away from him. He groans, rolling off of me.

"You're an evil one, you know," he complains.

"Oh come on, we both know what that full body massage later is code for."

I get back up, shoot him a sexy wink, and head back to the kitchen to grab my cup of coffee.

"Okay, I'm heading out! I've got a lot to do today!"

"Wait! One more kiss!" Tyson protests.

I grab my purse and my coffee and lean in like I'm about to kiss him. At the last second, I pull away and run outside, leaving him hanging.

"Evil!" he shouts after me.

"Save it for later!" I shout back, giggling on the way to my car.

Now it's time to get this show on the road. I have to find the missing final piece for my sculpture. Without really knowing where I'm heading, I begin driving around town.

I spend the entire morning and part of the afternoon stopping at random places and looking for anything that I might use. After a few hours, I've all but given up. I guess it's hard to find something when you have no idea what you're actually looking for.

Stopping at one more spot, with no luck, I get back in my car, exhausted from all my searching. I'm at a complete loss right now, and all I know is that I have got to take a break from this.

Completely discouraged, I decide to head over to the Muffin Top to get something sweet in me, hoping some cookies will reset my brain and I'll know exactly what I need. Maybe I'll even ask my sisters what they think. They're completely clueless about art, but sometimes fresh eyes can actually help.

Chapter Thirty-Two

As soon as Tru pulls out of the driveway to head to the warehouse, I gulp down my coffee, grab my keys and hop in my car. I'm going through with my plan to talk to her sisters about the situation to see what they think, or if they could offer me some help.

Once I arrive at the Muffin Top, I take a minute to make sure that I really want to do this. I don't want to potentially overstep by going to her sisters, but I really don't see any other option. Despite my nerves, I head inside anyway.

As soon as I walk in, Bridgid and Regina both notice me right away. I head to a booth in the corner and wave them over.

"Tyson, surprised to see you here," Bridgid remarks.

Though I know that what she really means is that she's surprised to see me here without Tru.

"Yeah, what's up? Everything okay?" Regina chimes in.

"Well, actually I came here because I needed some advice from you two."

"Hang on, we'll give you all the advice you want after we fill this table with some coffee and muffins," Bridgid cuts me off, and the two of them scuttle off behind the bakery counter.

They come back with a plate full of muffins, and three cups of coffee. I grab a chocolate chip muffin and knowing that B won't be satisfied until I do, I take a bite.

"Okay so what's going on, Ty?" Regina questions.

"It's about Trulia. I'm at a complete loss. To be frank with you… I'm in love with your sister. Have been since the moment we met. She brightens up my entire world. Trulia is everything I've ever wanted in a woman. I know without a doubt that that girl is my soulmate."

"Aww, Tyson that's so lovely to hear, it's about time she found someone… but wait, what's the problem then?"

"The problem is that I asked her to stay here in Belton with me, and she still hasn't given me an answer. I asked her to forego her apartment in New York, and officially move in with me. That was well over a week ago now, and neither of us have even so much as mentioned it since. But… since realizing that I'm fully in love with that girl… I can't just let her leave. She hasn't told me if she is going to go back to New York yet, but her lack of any response kind of makes me think that she isn't planning on staying. I'm not really sure what I expected from this, but I just really wanted to talk to you guys about this and I guess see what you thought."

"Wait so, you asked her to stay and then what? You guys just changed the subject?"

"Pretty much…"

"Okay well, here's the thing with Tru. If it's her idea— nothing will stop her from doing things. She definitely isn't afraid to take leaps. But when it comes to other people, she is. Basically, it has to be her idea. There's nothing you can say to make her change her mind; she has to come to that conclusion on her own."

"So… basically there's nothing I can do?"

My heart sinks.

"Not exactly. The thing is, you're already doing everything exactly the way you should be. You're giving her a safe, healthy, and happy environment. You're showing her what it truly feels like to be loved. All you can do is just continue to do that," Bridgid comforts me.

"But you have to understand that she isn't used to men being like you. Tru has never been with a guy that she could actually trust. She's never been in a relationship where she felt loved and welcomed all the time. More importantly, she's never been in a relationship where she had the chemistry that you two have. So as you can see, this is all new for her. Brand new. She is probably confused as hell, with no idea how to navigate all of these feelings she's having," Reggie explains.

"But the good thing is that she's still here. Look, if she didn't want to take you up on your offer, you better believe she would've skipped town as soon as you asked her. But she stayed… and that speaks volumes, trust me."

"She's right, it does. You'll learn over time that Trulia's actions speak way louder than her words. That's what makes her such an amazing artist. Trulia wants to stay here with you, she just hasn't admitted it to herself yet. But when she does, she'll tell you."

"So you guys think I should just wait? Give her some more time?"

"Yes, absolutely. But it wouldn't hurt if you were to tell her what you told us… that you're in love with her."

"Okay… well, I trust you guys. You know her better than she probably even knows herself. Thank you so much, really. You have no idea how much this means to me."

"Look, we just want our sister to be happy. It became very clear to us the moment we saw you two together that you make her happy, so we welcome you with open arms. Plus, she told us how Mama used to give you free samples—she doesn't give those to just anyone, so we automatically like you."

"Glad to hear that," I laugh.

"You can always come to us with all things involving Trulia. Even if we can't always give you the exact answer, we'll try to push you in the right direction."

They pack up some sweets for me and send me on my way, a little bit less confused than when I walked in. I don't feel one hundred percent better, but I definitely don't feel *completely* lost. I'm not sure exactly what I'm going to say to Trulia yet, but I head to the warehouse to see her anyway.

Chapter Thirty-Three

TRULIA

The second I walk into the Muffin Top; I notice something is off. Normally when I walk in, the place erupts. My sisters run up to me, babbling about how their days went. But today, it's completely silent. In fact, neither of them even say hello.

I think back to my last conversations with both of them, wondering if maybe I said something to anger either of them. I recall our last conversations being perfectly fine and normal, so it can't be that.

Maybe I was supposed to work a shift here today? I have a pretty shifty memory, it's entirely possible that I could forget that I was supposed to come in. I quickly check the calendar and don't see my name on the schedule, so it's not that either.

Maybe the two of them are fighting and that's why it's so quiet? But the two of them have been getting along so well lately.

Hmm. Guess I'll have to do a bit of digging.

"Hey you two! It's awfully quiet in here today," I remark.

Regina grunts and Bridgid nods. Neither of them say anything.

"Whatcha guys workin on?" I ask, noting that they're scooping some kind of dough onto some baking sheets.

"Trying out a new recipe for chocolate chip cookies," Bridgid answers.

"Really? But ours are already so good. People love them!"

"Yeah, I know—I just like to try out new recipes I find every now and then. You never know!"

"Makes sense, people are always coming up with new ways to make things. Well, I can't wait to try them!"

Again, no response. They don't even look up from the dough.

"Okay, spill," I state.

Enough beating around the bush.

"Huh?" Reggie questions, playing innocent.

"It's pretty obvious that you two are hiding something. So spill. What's the deal?"

They share a look with each other, but still don't say anything.

Fine. I'm not in the mood to play a guessing game. If they wanna keep secrets, then they can keep secrets. I grab a slice of my favorite chocolate satin pie and take a seat at the counter while they continue working. I eat my pie in silence, mulling over my current situation with Tyson.

"Everything okay with you?" Bridgid asks after a while.

"Um, yeah I'm fine. Just a little stressed out. I'm almost done with my tree sculpture, which is great and all… but there's something it's missing, and I just can't seem to figure out what that is. I've been searching all fucking day with no luck. I guess I'm just not used to not knowing exactly what my art needs, especially when it comes to the finishing touches."

Bridgid and Reggie share another look, before Bridgid turns back to me.

"Tru… is it at all possible that maybe you're using this as an excuse to not finish your sculpture because you secretly don't want it to be done?"

"Why would I do that?" I'm not exactly sure where she's going with this.

"Well… as long as your sculpture still needs work—then you have a reason to stay in town…"

"Aaand why would I need a reason to stay in town?"

"I'm just saying—maybe it's possible?"

"That I'm purposely not accepting that my project is finished because I don't want to go back to New York?"

She nods.

Before responding further, I think about it for a moment. I have *never* purposely not finished a project before. In fact, once it gets to a certain point—I'm usually in a huge rush to finish it. But the more I think about it—the more likely it seems.

Thinking about my sculpture, I realize that it *is* done, and that it probably has been for a while now. It's beautiful, and it's completely perfect. It doesn't need anything else. But… Why would I be putting this off? It doesn't make any sense.

"Maybe you're right…" I confess. "But why would I do that? Why would I use this as an excuse to stay? I'm a grown woman, if I wanna stay I can stay."

Reggie finally speaks up.

"Well… maybe because you don't want to admit to yourself that the *real* reason you want to stay is because you're in love with a *certain* handyman…"

"You think… you think I'm in love with Tyson?"

"Aren't you?" Bridgid questions, her brow furrowing.

Me, in love with Tyson… what a scary thought. But is it true? Honestly, I haven't thought much about it. Okay that's a lie. I have definitely associated my feelings for Tyson with the word love before.

When I picture his face in my head, my heartbeat quickens, and my stomach fills with butterflies. When I think about going home to him after a long day in the warehouse, I feel excitement. When I hear his car pulling up outside while I'm working on my project, I forget about everything else but him. I am definitely in love with this man.

I am completely, one hundred percent in love with Tyson Michael Hayes. So why haven't I admitted this until today? After some thinking, I come to the conclusion that I'm scared to commit to this because I have never actually been in any kind of serious relationship like this before. When it comes to relationships, I have always avoided the more serious, long term commitments.

This is all new to me. I've never felt this strongly about a man. I've never been this sure about a man. Tyson is the first man I have ever been in love with.

Having finally admitted all of this to myself, I begin to wonder if Tyson even feels the same way that I do. What if he doesn't? I can't just assume the feelings are mutual.

No. Tyson definitely loves me, I have no doubt about that. He has never made me question the way he feels about me. Not many women can say that about the man they love.

Abandoning my pie, I stand up and grab my purse.

"Hey uh, thanks for the talk guys, it really helped. But there's something I need to go do."

With that, I leave the bakery, get in my car, and head home… to Tyson's.

Chapter Thirty-Four

TYSON

After a couple hours of hanging around the warehouse, cleaning and organizing the place while waiting for an absent Trulia to show up—I head home. I'm completely exhausted and ready to just relax for the rest of the day. Honestly, Tru might be on her own for dinner tonight— I'm too tired to even cook anything.

The drive home is a blur, I'm surprised I even made it all in one piece. Once I arrive, I grab the mail, unlock the door, and walk inside, only to be completely stunned. The mail falls out of my hands and onto the floor. My jaw drops.

Standing before me is a beautiful, lingerie clad Trulia. Her straight, shiny black hair hangs past her waist. She

197

wears a red satin bra, and red satin high waisted crotchless panties with sheer lace along the sides. The rest of her body is completely naked. She has no makeup on, save for her trademark cherry red lips.

I can't help but stare at her, until I notice my surroundings. Candles completely cover the foyer and the hallway leading to our bedroom. I look back at her.

"What a—what's going on here?" I question.

A sexy, wicked smile spreads across her perfect lips as she saunters up to me, hips swaying back and forth. She stares into my eyes, still smiling as she begins to unbutton my shirt. She maintains eye contact until my shirt is off and begins running her hands along my torso.

Unable to resist, I reach out for her, but she immediately backs away, the evil smile returning. She wags her finger at me, takes my hand and leads me to the bedroom. Once again, I'm struck by how much I love her. The entire way there, all I can think about is how I can't wait to tell this woman how I feel. But… first things first, of course.

Once there, she turns to me and begins pulling off the rest of my clothes until I'm standing in front of her completely naked. Her hands run along my body, teasing me until I almost can't bear it any longer.

Just when I think I can't take it anymore, she pushes me down onto the bed, straddling me. She trails kisses all over my body until she reaches my lips. As soon as our lips touch, every nerve in my body comes alive. My cock aches, needing her.

She grinds against me, teasing me all over again.

"Please," I whisper. "I need you."

A satisfied smile spreads across her face this time, as if that were all she was waiting to hear this entire time, and she turns around into a reverse cowgirl position. She looks back at me, as she massages my cock, teasing the tip of it at her entrance before turning back around and sliding me all the way into her.

We moan together, and I grab onto her hips as she rides me, closing my eyes and letting myself feel everything. I feel not only the pleasure of being inside of her, but the pleasure of knowing that I'm in love with her all at the same time.

She hops up and down on my dick, while I grip her skin and slap her plump ass. I rock myself up into her as hard as I can, needing more and more of her. We come together, screaming out in pleasure. I've never come so hard in my life, and yet somehow, I still need her.

It's my turn to take control. I flip her around onto her back, place her legs up on my shoulders and plunge myself into her.

"*Fuck*, Tyson," she groans.

As I fuck her, I grasp her breasts, pulling her silk bra down to reveal her erect nipples. Teasing one in between my fingers, I lick the other before taking it into my mouth, pinching it in between my teeth. She screams out and digs her nails into the skin on my back.

I become lost in her, completely forgetting about anything except how amazing she feels. I speed up, pounding into her despite having already finished once again. I'm sure her screams are being heard all the way down the block, but I don't care. All I care about right now is making the woman I love come. And I do. Multiple times.

Chapter Thirty-Five

TRULIA

Turns out my idea to surprise Tyson in my best lingerie when he got home was the best idea I've had yet. I've already had three orgasms and edging towards a fourth at this very moment.

Tyson's head is between my thighs. He grips my ass with both hands, clutching at me as he flicks his tongue across my clit in all the right spots. I've never actually been with a man that was good at oral before Tyson. Looks like I have definitely won the lottery with this one.

He works two of his fingers inside of me, massaging them against my g-spot as his tongue works on my clit. It isn't long before I'm clutching at his hair, back arched and screaming out his name as I hit that fourth orgasm.

He collapses next to me, both of us catching our breath. I'm in such a haze, it takes me a few minutes to come back down to earth. But once I do, I'm ready for more. I get out of bed, strip off my lingerie, and head to the shower.

"You coming?" I call back to Tyson.

Of course he is. What kind of man resists shower sex?

I turn the hot water all the way up, and the bathroom steams up almost immediately. We get in together and begin soaping each other up. He lathers my body, massaging every inch of me. Once I'm covered in soap, he turns me around and begins washing my hair.

He massages my scalp with his fingers while working the soap in. It's such a sensual and intimate experience, and I can feel our bond growing even more by the second. Once he rinses the soap out of my hair, he turns me back around so that I'm facing him. He takes my breasts in his hands, massaging my nipples with his fingers, while leaning in to kiss me.

I moan into his lips, surrendering myself to him once again. Beginning to massage his cock, I break away from the kiss and get down on my knees. I continue to jerk him as I bring my lips to his balls, taking them in my mouth.

Playing with his balls, I suck on them, tease them, and massage them in between my lips, while he groans, enjoying every minute of it. Finally, I bring my mouth up to his shaft, licking him up and down.

I look up at him as I plunge him down my throat, so I can see that look of pure pleasure in his eyes. Cupping his balls in my hands, I play with them once again while I suck his dick until he comes in my mouth.

As soon as he finishes, he yanks me up by my hair, swivels me around and slams me up against the wall, pushing my head against the tile. He massages my pussy before shoving himself in. I scream out, clutching at the walls, never fully used to how big he is.

He slaps my ass as hard as he can, causing me to shriek in pain. Ignoring my shriek, he grabs hold of my neck, pulling it back until my head is resting against his chest as he fucks me, while keeping a firm grip around my throat.

I lose myself in the ecstasy, trying not to finish before he does. Try as I might, I lose my internal battle and come on his dick. Tyson doesn't skip a beat, continuing to fuck me until this time we finish together.

I turn around, pressing my body against his. We stand there, water running over us, embracing each other for what feels like hours. I consider saying it in this moment, that I love him. But I don't want him to confuse my love for lust.

Once we finish cleaning up, we dry each other off and head back to bed, cuddling up to each other under the covers. He kisses my forehead softly, caressing my face. I stare at him, mesmerized. Everything about him is so perfect.

After awhile, Tyson turns to lay on his back, and I snuggle up into the crook of his arm. It's then that I decide I can't hold it in any longer, and it tumbles out of me before I can chicken out again.

"Tyson… there's something I need to tell you. I've been wanting to say this for some time now, but I only just admitted it to myself today. I love you… I'm in love with you Ty, and I want to spend the rest of my life with you…"

I hold my breath waiting for a response, but it never comes. Fuck… I misinterpreted—he doesn't actually love me back…

After a minute goes by, I work up the nerve to look over at him, but when I do I realize that Tyson is sound asleep.

Goddamnit.

I mentally smack myself for wearing him out so much that I didn't even get to tell him. Tonight was supposed to be *the* night.

Fuck.

Sighing, I snuggle back up to him and join him in his slumber.

Chapter Thirty-Six

TYSON

When I wake up, I feel something missing before I even open my eyes. It only takes a slight twitch of my arm to realize Trulia isn't next to me anymore. I reach around the sheets further to see if she just rolled over sometime last night, but the linen is cold. So… she's gone. I would be worried if this didn't happen a lot.

The behavior isn't exactly unusual. She can be slippery, evasive. For all I know, she may have just gone to work on a project or could even be out in the front of my house. Sighing, I roll out of my bed. I put on a t-shirt and some pants before walking out into the hallway.

Right when my feet hit the cold floor, I regret not putting some socks on, too, but I don't feel like turning around, so I keep on and pray that my toes will acclimate soon. The rest of the house is empty, though, from the kitchen to the bathroom.

So Trulia's definitely out of the house.

Since I'm in the bathroom anyway, I go ahead and clean up before heading back downstairs, still thinking about why Trulia left so quickly without telling me.

Thinking back to last night, I think I heard Trulia whispering something to me as I fell asleep— gosh, I was tired— but I can't remember what she had been saying for the life of me. Maybe it was nothing at all?

No, it has to be something. I guess I just don't know what. I guess I'll just have to ask her when she gets back, whenever that is. Once I'm done, I leave the bathroom and head downstairs into the kitchen.

Then I put on the coffee pot. As soon as I press the start button, my phone begins to ring. I turn around and see Trulia's beautiful face on the screen. I can't help but perk up as I pick the phone up and answer.

"Hey," I say, "I got up a bit ago and noticed you were gone."

"Yeah, I had to leave quickly," Trulia answers. I can tell she's out of breath by how she answers, each syllable accompanied by a heave.

"Last night was nice, wasn't it?" I find my smile widening as I say it to her, feeling proud of both of us. And to think we had thought we weren't going to make it before.

"Um… yeah, it was fine— one minute, Tyson." I hear her voice move away from the phone. Wherever she is must be very loud. Even though her voice is fuzzy, I can still hear her yelling. *"Sorry, what did you say?"*

"Hey, where are you?" I ask her. "It seems a little busy."

"Busy? Yeah, I am." She must have misheard me a little.

"No, I said where are you, Trulia? Are you still in town?"

"I can't hear you right now. Give me a minute." I listen to more muffled static as she travels through wherever she is. I really can't tell where. Maybe she's in the town square or the grocery store. I can't imagine anywhere else I wouldn't be able to hear her.

"Trulia?" I say into the phone after the line goes silent. "Trulia? Are you still there?"

"Yeah, sorry." Wherever she is it's quieter now. She's still breathing heavily but a little less so. And the background noise is still there but not as pronounced. *"I'm back, Tyson."*

"What's going on? Are you at the store or something? It's really loud," I say.

"No, no. I'm actually about to leave."

"Leave? Are you all right?"

"I'm fine." I wait for her to continue, but she doesn't.

"Where are you, then?"

"Oh my gosh— Well, there's some… My— I don't have time to explain it right now. There was an emergency over in New York with my apartment, so I have to catch a flight and go back right now. I'm at the airport."

"Your apartment? I thought you were subletting it."

"I was— I am— but I'm the original leasee, so I have to be the one to handle it."

"Oh, what's the emergency? Can I help at all?"

"No, there's really nothing you can do."

"So, when—" I want to ask her when she thinks she'll be back, but I'm not sure it's the right question to ask at this moment. "—never mind, it's not important. Hopefully you get things sorted out. Let me know if you need anything."

"Listen, Tyson, I have to go right now. I don't have any time."

"Yeah, yeah, sure. By—" The line goes dead before I can even finish. "Bye, Trulia," I say out loud to myself. I feel my heart sinking. She's leaving. Right when it feels like we've found a groove she's leaving.

I'm starting to wonder if she stayed more than a month just to go back. Why didn't she wake me before she left? She said it wasn't planned, but maybe it was, maybe she found out last night and just didn't tell me for some reason. Or maybe I'm just forgetting…

Cracking my knuckles, I run through everything she's said to me since we got back together. I can't remember her mentioning her apartment beyond the sublease, and nothing about New York. The only words she's said that I can't remember are last nights.

Sinking into a kitchen chair, I wonder if everything she did last night was just to say goodbye to me. Has she always known she was going to fly back to New York and not come back? Did she care enough about me to give one last good time before disappearing?

I wasted my time by not telling her how I felt, didn't I?

I slam my fist against the table, not knowing what else to do. I feel all this pain welling up in my chest, a leak from the hole she left in my heart.

I don't think I'll be able to fix this.

Chapter Thirty-Seven

TRULIA

"Listen, Tyson, I have to go right now. I don't have any time," I say, hanging up the phone.

"I know, I know," I say to the airport security guard as I throw my phone into the bin. He's been telling me, but I've been trying to finish my call with Tyson. I feel bad about not being able to stay on longer, but I need to hurry before I'm late for my flight, and I can't stand behind the checkpoint any longer, especially with this long line.

I put the rest of my belongings into the bag and take my shoes off. Then I walk through in line. I have this anxious pit in my stomach for whatever is awaiting me in New York.

I woke up to a call from the New York City Police. Apparently, James, my— sort of boyfriend?— showed up drunk at my apartment last night. He'd been looking for me. I haven't been answering his calls, so I could see why, but I thought he knew I was here in my hometown.

Of course, he found the guy I've been subleasing the house to, and from there it escalated pretty quickly. Not listening to reason, James thought this guy was someone else and destroyed my apartment in some drunken rage.

He broke half of the furniture, a few of the walls, and half of the dishes. I think I'll have a pretty solid case to get back the value, but I'll still have to buy all new things. This is all happening at the wrong time.

Even though I'm here in Texas and the sublessee is there, the police are still insisting that I have to come and press charges against James since the property that was destroyed in the apartment is mine and my landlord's not the sublessee's. This, of course, just makes things that much more complicated for me.

It's just my luck that James has managed to make my life a living hell yet again. You'd think he somehow sensed that I was happy when he showed up drunk at my place. That's not even the worst part, though.

Painstakingly, I had to leave Tyson behind and book a last-minute flight, something that hurts my heart and my checkbook. I need to get to New York as soon as I can, though, so there's no time to wait.

I didn't even have time to tell Tyson, all the questions he always has about everything. If that phone call we just had proves anything, it's that. I need to go to New York and cut ties with the city for good.

I let out a small grunt as I pick up my bags and continue through the airport. For a small moment, I consider calling Tyson back and explaining things in more detail, but something tells me I still wouldn't have the time to give him the answers he wants, so I decide to hold off at least until I land in New York.

I don't have any bags to check, so I begin towards my gate. Checking the clock on my phone, I see I have a little time until my flight. Still, I hurry to my gate just to make sure I'm not late.

As soon as I take a seat, I feel my phone buzzing in my pocket. Bridgid's face lights up on the screen. Immediately, I remember we're supposed to be doing brunch… right now. Wincing, I pick up the phone.

"Hey, Bridgid."

"Hey, where are you?"

"The airport. I'm about to board my flight." Checking my ticket, I see that I'm in the last boarding group. "I think I have a little time but not a lot."

"What happened to brunch?"

"I know… I know, I'm sorry. I just… There's stuff going on at my apartment. James showed up, and he ended up trashing my apartment."

"Can't your sublessee handle it?"

"That's what I thought, but apparently not since the contract is between me and my landlord. That's why I'm here."

"That's too bad. Did Tyson come with you?"

"No, I left without him."

"Have you talked at all?"

"We talked a bit but not much. He had too many questions, and I was going through security. I'll call him later, but right now I need to go." I look at the gate and see the last of the people going through. "Actually, I'm going to board. I'll talk to you later, Bridgid, okay?"

"Sure, sure, go get on your flight. I'll talk to you later."

I hang up the phone and slip through right before the flight attendant closes the gate. Breathing a sigh of relief, I walk at a slower pace as I board the plane and take a seat. I'm thankful I was able to get an aisle seat this late.

Now that I have time to sit, I'm thinking back to the phone call with Tyson. It's making me realize that I'm more than ready to settle down back here in my hometown. When I was younger, I couldn't have even imagined staying.

That's how I ended up in New York in the first place. But now I can't imagine anywhere but home to live and start this next chapter in my life. New York has been fun, but I'm ready to put it all behind me. I was already planning to before this whole thing with James happened.

Even though I'm just leaving, I'm already anxious to get back to Belton, back to Tyson. Damn, I should've gone ahead and called him in the few minutes I had before the gate. If not to answer his questions then at least to reassure him that we're okay, especially since I know I didn't phrase things the best during that quick phone call.

He probably thinks I'm mad at him and doesn't even know when I'm coming back. I've screwed this up, haven't I? Closing my eyes, I know I can't do anything right now.

I'll fix it when I get to New York.

Until then, I'll just have to sit for the ride.

Chapter Thirty-Eight

TYSON

"You can't just wait at the phone," I tell myself, still in the kitchen at the table.

It's been about fifteen minutes since Trulia hung up on me, so I know it's not likely she's going to be returning my call anytime soon.

Still, that doesn't make me any less anxious about it. I throw my head back and pinch the corners of my eyes. Why couldn't she have just told me right then?

It seemed like she was avoiding me altogether. She hasn't left any of her belongings here. For all I know, she won't be coming back here. She'll call me back, say things are taking longer than expected, and then fade off via text or something.

I can't let that happen, though. I… I love her too much for that.

Of course, this is all just in my head. She could just be going to New York for an emergency. I don't even know if her ticket is one way or round trip. She could be coming back tomorrow or the day after that.

Really, she hasn't said anything that is a true red flag. This is all just based on inferences, isn't it? And those aren't facts.

I know I'm overthinking this, but that doesn't make me any less anxious.

"I need to just get up and go," I say out loud, finally standing from my seat. Having forgotten my coffee, I pour a cold cup of it and stick it in the microwave for a minute while fishing a loaf of bread and a few eggs from my pantry and fridge.

There's not one part of me that's hungry right now, but I know I need to do something until my mind can be eased. I don't even know how long a flight to New York is or how long it would take her to get to a place where she can call me. So I guess I'll just be waiting for an update whenever it can be given.

As I sit down with my coffee and toast (I decided to nix the eggs), I realize this may not be the best plan for the day. Maybe I should reschedule some of my repair calls? I had planned on spending it with Trulia, but now that I'm not, I need something to keep me busy.

I pick up my phone and go to the calendar app. Looking at my upcoming projects, it seems like there isn't really anything for me to do anyway. Business is always slow this time of year, and I still need to work on getting some of the clients I lost after the warehouse robbery.

"So that's a no go." I sigh and set my phone back down. Taking a bite out of my toast, I stare out into space. It isn't long before I start trying to think about what I'll do if she doesn't come back.

My phone buzzes. I startle and pick it up, hoping it's Trulia, but it's just a spam email. Grunting, I set it back down yet again. This happens a few more times until I finally hear my ringtone. My eyes light up until I see it's just Alex. I answer anyway.

"Hello?"

"Hey, dude. What's up with you?"

"Nothing really. Just waiting."

"What're you waiting for?"

"Trulia had some emergency in New York and had to fly back. She was in a rush, so we didn't get to talk fully. I don't know why, but I just have a bad feeling about the whole situation."

"I thought you guys were back together and good."

"We are— I mean, we were. Like I said, I'm not so sure anymore. She was saying something to me last night that I didn't catch, and then she didn't wake me up when she was leaving this morning. I'm trying to figure out why she didn't say goodbye or anything. It's weird. And I don't have any jobs scheduled for today, so I'm really just sitting here thinking about it."

"That's too bad. I'd come over if I weren't at work right now. Maybe later. You shouldn't just sit there, though. Go do something."

"Like what? I don't want to leave the house."

"Then read a book, watch a movie. Don't just sit at the phone like a puppy or something. You won't miss the call whenever she gets back to you."

"I guess…." I let out a deep sigh as I run a hand through my hair. "Well I don't want to keep you. Talk to you later, Alex."

"Yeah, Ty." The line clicks as it ends.

After sitting there for a moment, I realize there's someone else I can call for more details. I dial Bridgid and listen to the ring.

"Hello?"

"Hey, Bridgid."

"Oh, hey, Tyson. How are you?"

"I'm fine. Have you heard anything from Trulia?"

"Trulia? No, why? I thought she was with you. I mean, we're going for brunch in a bit, but I doubt she's left yet."

"She told me she's flying to New York to handle an emergency. She didn't tell you?"

"Um, no… Are you sure?"

"Yeah, she left this morning before I woke up. I got a chance to talk to her for a minute, but she wasn't able to give any details. I know you girls are close, so I thought she might've called you."

"I'm sorry, Tyson, but I don't know anything about that. And I doubt Regina does either. I may have to try calling her if she doesn't show."

"Sounds like a good idea. I'm about to call her again right now in case she has a moment. If she does call you, do you mind letting me know?"

"Of course."

"Okay, thanks, Bridgid. Bye."

After Bridgid hangs up, I'm pressing Trulia's number. The trill of the phone goes once… twice… three times…

Voicemail. Damn it.

I don't bother leaving her a message and just press the red button to end the call.

What the hell is going on?

Chapter Thirty-Nine

TRULIA

The moment the plane lands, I'm already unbuckling my seatbelt and readying myself to get off board. Usually, I'm the type to sit in my seat and finish a movie while the rest of the passengers exit, but today, I really just want to go.

The sooner I can finish with all of this, the sooner I can go home. I know I still need to call Tyson, but I know I still don't have time. As I file out of the plane, I decide I'll call him later after the police are gone and everything is more settled.

At least then I won't be as tense and snap at him like I did on our last call. As I roll my suitcase through the airport and look around, I realize how alone I feel. Big city, thousands of people, one of me.

Usually New York feels just right when I come back, like my true home where I can be free and express myself. But today it just feels empty. All the people I love are back home now.

"Well, I'm not going to miss it here," I say, standing at the crosswalk.

"Are you from here?" a woman who's also waiting asks me. She seems bright eyed, adventurous. I know that's how excited I must have looked my first time flying here.

"Sort of. I'm from Texas, but I've lived here the past 15 years. This'll probably be my last time coming for a while, though. I'm relocating."

"Oh, what do you do?"

"I'm an artist."

"That's amazing. I just moved here to do ballet."

"It's a wonderful place," I tell her as we walk across the crossed lines in the street.

"Then why are you leaving?"

"Um, everything I have is back home."

"I see. Well, good luck."

"You too!" I break off to the line and go to the left. I know the path to my apartment vaguely, but it feels so foreign. I know I haven't been gone that long, but it feels as if it's been an eternity.

Right when I get the front of my apartment building, I feel this cloud come over me. I've never felt such a foreboding energy, but I've also never returned to New York to place a police report.

"Damn, James," I sigh as I enter. My stomach knots up more and more as I stand in the elevator and ride to my floor. By the time I'm unlocking the door to my place, I've calmed myself. But the moment I see the mess, I feel sick again.

James didn't just destroy the furniture or the appliances. I see the remnants of several years' worth of artwork strewn all over the floor, from my torn canvases to shattered ceramics. He ruined everything.

Everything.

I don't know what a police report is going to do about this. He destroyed everything I worked so hard for. These pieces are priceless. It's not like I can buy my first bust again. Sure, I can purchase the paints, but no amount of money could recreate what I had built.

I don't blame the sublessee for finding somewhere else to stay. James really has trashed the place. I never would have expected something like that from someone like him.

He was always so chill. He never yelled, never got upset. He was always the guy breaking up fights in bars and getting along with everyone. I used to think that if you couldn't get along with James, you couldn't get along with anyone.

Clearly, that's not the case. Did something change, or has he just had me fooled this entire time? It's not like there was much of a chance for us when I got back, but there definitely isn't now.

Sliding against the wall in the foyer, I sink down into a crouch, my fingers at either side of my temple. It's just so much. What am I going to do?

I startle when I hear a knock at the door.

"Police."

"Oh, come on in. It's Katrina Grant, the owner." I stand and pull the door wider to let the police officer into my apartment.

"Ms. Grant, I'm Officer Warren. I need to get a report together of all that Mr. Robert destroyed. Do you plan on pressing charges?"

"Yes, but I don't know how much good that's going to do."

"Any compensation is something," he says, pulling his notepad out.

"I know, I know. But some of this stuff can't be replaced, you know?"

"I understand. You're an artist?"

"Yep." I shrug. "Anyway, I guess we can get started. Do you want to begin in the front or the back?"

"Let's start in the front and work our way back. Then I can read to you the witness statement as we go."

Going through the apartment and the damages with the officer is like an out of body experience. I'm there, but everything I'm describing, and everything the officer is saying to me, feels dead, numb.

As soon as he's done, I escort him out of the apartment, a long sigh leaving my body as I go to the couch and take a seat on it, exhaustion creeping up my spine and bubbling like a bad taste in the back of my throat.

I hunch over, my elbows digging into my thighs. I don't know where to go from here. Do I stay until I can finish pressing charges on James, or do I go back home and then just fly back for the court date? Of course, that's if we have court. James may want to settle.

A part of me wants to call him, but I know it wouldn't be wise. Then I'm thinking—is this how I made Tyson feel when I left the warehouse unlocked and it got robbed? If so, I can see why he had been so mad.

Tears fill my eyes as I lay on my side and pull my legs up onto the couch, in the midst of destruction. I cry myself to sleep.

Chapter Forty

Tyson

I punch in the code that Bridgid gave me for Trulia's apartment building in New York, and let myself in. I haven't heard from her since that short phone call before she boarded her flight, and by the end of the next day, I was worried sick—so I got the soonest flight out and came to New York.

I'm not sure exactly what's going on, but whatever it is, I just felt like I needed to come here and find out. I couldn't just sit at home wondering, psyching myself out. I couldn't take another minute of worrying about her or worrying that I did something to lose her. So, here I am.

I walk up two flights of stairs, and find apartment 313, knocking on the door. After a few seconds, I hear the sound of feet shuffling and the door unlocks and opens, revealing a haggard Trulia and a completely destroyed apartment behind her.

Her tear-streaked face turns from depressed to complete shock. I pull her towards me into a tight hug, shutting the door behind us. Trulia immediately dissolves into tears, sobbing into my chest. I hold her, rubbing her back and waiting for her to calm down to find out what happened.

Once she starts to calm down, she leads me over to her couch, the only thing that appears to be left in one piece. We sit down, and she proceeds to tell me everything that happened.

"This guy that I had been seeing before I left New York —James—did this. I guess he came over to my apartment to see me—even though he knew that I was in Texas— and when he got here, he was met with the guy that was subleasing my apartment. I guess he must have thought that I was cheating on him with the guy or something, so he came in and started screaming at him, while completely destroying the place. My sublessee called the cops and left immediately, finding another place to stay. That's why I had to come out here so quickly, the cops needed me to make a statement of everything that was destroyed. I had to be here to press charges against James."

Without saying anything, I pull her towards me. I can' even imagine how she's feeling right now. As I look around, I notice that it's not just furniture that's destroyed—there are paintings slashed, pottery and sculptures smashed and strewn all over the place. I clutch her tighter.

"He ruined everything, Tyson… this is my life's work here. All of my most prized pieces… gone."

She begins to sob all over again, becoming more frantic. It becomes clear to me that I need to say something to help her, and quick.

"Trulia… look at me. This is horrible, and I can't even imagine what you must be feeling right now—but listen to me. Your life still has meaning without this stuff, okay? Just because it's all gone, doesn't mean it never existed. I know that you're an artist, and I'm not, so I can't possibly understand what it's like to lose everything you've created… but look at it like this—now you can start fresh. You can come back home to Belton and make all new art that will *never* be destroyed. I will hire a personal bodyguard to stand outside the warehouse and protect your art if I have to."

She giggles through her subsided tears, smiling up at me.

"Tru… when you left, I was worried *sick* about you. I just knew something was wrong, and I was so scared that I had lost you. That's why I came here. I couldn't bare the thought of losing you… because I love you Trulia. I'm in love with you, and I have been since the day we met in that railyard. You're my soulmate, my person. I need you."

Finally confessing this feels like five hundred pounds have been lifted off of my shoulders. I feel free, like there's nothing holding me back.

"Oh, Tyson… I don't ever want you to be scared that you're going to lose me again, ever. Because I'm in love with you too. I was trying to tell you that the night before I left, but you had already fallen asleep. I would *never* just up and leave forever without even saying goodbye, okay? I don't want you to ever think that again. The truth is, I've been planning to stay in Belton for a while now, I was just scared to take that leap. But now I'm not. I'm officially moving back home and never leaving again unless it's with you."

Utterly ecstatic to hear those words come out of her mouth, I immediately pull her into a deep kiss. I love this girl so much, and I don't ever have to wonder if she feels the same way again. She's mine, all mine.

Trulia and I hire some people to pack up whatever can be salvaged from her apartment and send it to my—*our* house in Texas. We fly back home where we set out to live the rest of our lives with each other, in the small, quirky town that brought us together. I know in my heart that it truly doesn't matter where we are, as long as she's with me. I guess home really *is* where the heart is…

I hope you enjoyed Trulia and Tyson's story! Looking for more BWWM Interracial Romance? Check out the **UnReal Marriage** series of standalone stories…

1-4. The Fake Fiancé Boxed Set One - http://bklink.to/ffbox-buy

5-8. The Fake Fiancé Boxed Set Two - http://bklink.to/ffbox2-buy

9. The Contestant's Fake Fiancé - http://bklink.to/contestant-buy

10. The Reporter's Fake Fiancé - http://bklink.to/reporter-buy

Or how about some Black Queen's who rule New York City's club scene? Grab the **Sistaz Club** boxed set today! http://bklink.to/sistazbox-buy

About the Author

Hey readers! I'm Tasha Hart, author of contemporary romances. Thanks for reading my stories. From a young age, I've been inspired to tell stories about the ideas I have all the time. It started with telling wild stories, then some wilding of my own... but now I'm settling down with some good coffee and trying to write great books. It's a lot like running, which is what I usually do to figure out how my characters are going to misbehave. Totally distracting, consumes me wholly in the moment, and then it feels like magic! If you like reading my stories, consider pushing the Amazon follow button so you'll get notified when I've got a new book release!

Find Tasha online at… https://tashahart.com